MW00935789

The Long Journey
Christian Historical Fiction

By

Cliff Ball

Copyright © 2015
Published by Cliff Ball
The Long Journey
Christian historical fiction
Book 1 of An American Journey
Visit cliffball.net

ISBN-13: 978-1508942665
ISBN-10: 1508942668

Chapter 1

It was the shouting that woke George up.

"George! George! Wake up! Get out of bed!"

Realizing that he was the one being shouted at, George kept his eyes closed and asked, "Huh? What?"

"You've got to get up. The Army's here, or it's the Georgia militia, I can't tell. They want everyone outside,"

"Why?"

"Don't you remember? That Major General, Winfield Scott, was sent here to finally remove us to that so-called Indian Territory out west. Looks as if that's happening now,"

Not good news, George thought to himself while getting groggily out of bed. He glanced at John, his only brother, who looked like he had just gotten out bed himself, and asked, "What time is it?"

"It's close to sunrise. The sun hasn't come over the horizon yet, but they're insisting everyone get up now and gather outside. So hurry up, brother!"

"All right, all right, I'm coming."

While getting dressed by the light of his oil lamp in middle October 1838, George prayed, "Heavenly Father, please help my people and I deal with those who wish to remove us from our lands, the lands of my ancestors. I ask for the strength to do what is right in your sight. Thank you for all that you do for us, including dying for my sins. In your name, I pray, amen."

Christian missionaries came to the village in 1828 to establish a church for his little clan of Cherokees in what was now northern Georgia. George accepted Christ into his heart at ten years old and his family had done the same. His parents and the clan changed their names to anglicized versions and took the last name of the missionaries, Massey, for their own. George took his first and middle name after the first President of the United States and John took the name of the second President. The missionary family left the now established church to his parents, and his father had led their clan's church services up until he and his mother died from cholera five years earlier. George was now in charge of the church and was also the leader of the clan at the age of twenty.

The fact that his clan were Christians didn't matter to the last two American administrations, Andrew Jackson previously and now Martin Van Buren, who viewed all Indians as savages or potential enemies of the United States. Settlers in increasing numbers wanted the lands of the five tribes and religious affiliation hardly mattered at all. While his people were Christians, George's father had insisted that they remain true to their culture. The Indian Removal Act of 1830 was enacted to remove tribes who didn't want to assimilate into American society. George heard about the Seminoles in Florida who were at war with the United States over this very issue. In George's clan, almost all of the young people under the age of thirty left voluntarily years earlier to Indian Territory, which left him and John with thirty older people, all of whom were over fifty. Now the day had arrived when leaving was not voluntary.

Grabbing day old bread off the table so he'd have something to eat, George went outside to meet with Major General Scott. Scott and his men were on horseback, and his men had their guns pointed at the people gathered. George hoped to keep the tensions down so no one would get killed. He approached Scott, and asked, "Are we being forced to leave now? The sun has barely come up,"

"Are you in charge here?"

"Yes, I suppose you could say that,"

"Good. You and your people have been ordered by the United States government to leave and make your way to Indian Territory. We have other Cherokee waiting for your little group, so it would be best if we get on our way immediately,"

"We need to gather up food and other supplies before we make the journey. Surely you'd allow us to do that, sir,"

"I can't allow that. I have my orders to remove you and that's what we're going to do. By force, if we have to,"

"But what about the fact that the Supreme Court ruled that the United States couldn't force us to leave?"

"As President Jackson once said, 'I'd like to see them try to enforce that ruling.' Besides, your own Cherokee government signed a treaty that gives up their lands, so you have no legal leg to stand on, young man. If you keep resisting, we will remove you by force. These men with me are Georgia militia and would have no problem showing you they mean business. Am I correct, men?"

The men responded positively, with some tossing of racial slurs at the Cherokee assembled. Scott seemed greatly amused by what was happening, and said, "Maybe we ought to show them we mean business. Torch a house."

Three militiamen on horseback headed for the nearest house with a torch that was already lit. Before George could do or say anything, John ran in front of the horses to try to block the men from getting any closer to the house to burn it down. John wasn't a warrior, but he stood proudly as he attempted to stop them.

"You can't do this. It's not the Christian thing to do. We're all God's children, why defy Him by harming us? What did we ever do to you? Please stop."

"Stupid savage," said one of the men as he fired his rifle at John. The bullet hit John squarely in the chest and he was dead before he hit the ground.

"No!" shouted George, but before he could run over to his brother's side to check on him, two militiamen grabbed him and held onto him. Tears began flowing down his cheek as he mourned for his brother and how alone he felt, with both parents and now, his brother, dead. But, he was comforted in the thought that he would see his brother in Heaven someday.

"Do you see what happens when you defy us? Men, torch the house. Now, will you leave by your own power or do we need to kill you too?"

Wiping away tears, George replied, "We'll go, you'll get no more trouble from us."

"Excellent. Follow us as we lead you to the other members of your tribe, and then you'll get to travel to Indian Territory together."

The thirty clan members followed George out of their village with only the clothes on their backs and with very little food. Winter was near and there was a chill in the air. He heard Scott's men laughing as they plundered each house and then torched them too. The heavy smoke from the village being burned down drifted over the travelers. Looking back, George could see the smug look on Scott's face, which both angered and saddened him. His fleshly nature wanted to attack the much older man and kill him, while his spiritual side felt sorry for Scott, and he hoped that the General knew Christ as his Lord and Savior.

I hope he prays for forgiveness for this sin he's committing if he is a Christian, Lord, and if he's not, I hope he is led to you soon. George thought while praying, *Dear Lord God in Heaven, please guide me on this journey and lead my people to safety. I pray that we find success in the new lands and you bless us in everything we do in your name. Thy will be done. In your name, I pray, amen.*

Hours later, with the rising sun at their backs, the thirty-one members of the Massey clan arrived where many other Cherokee were being held in what looked like a corral before they were to travel west. George hadn't been looking forward to meeting other tribe members. Many of those who remained in the lands viewed his clan as more white than Indian, since they had become Christians and appeared to be assimilated, so the few felt that the Massey clan had betrayed the overall Cherokee nation. This was in spite of John Ross, the chief of the whole Cherokee nation, being a Christian too and having assimilated into the American ways. The whites, George felt, saw him and all Cherokees as savage Indians and nothing more. If he'd had been honest with himself, George would admit that he really didn't feel like he fit in with either culture, but since he couldn't do anything about it, he tried to never give it much thought.

The Massey clan stood a few feet away from the main group, mostly because of the looks of hatred and mistrust coming from some of their fellow Cherokee. The group nearest to George were obviously the members of the nation who wanted nothing to do with the white man's ways. George knew some even wanted war. However, without guns, tomahawks, or other weapons of war, they could do nothing about it. For now, the clan kept away from the others the best they could since the long journey to Indian Territory would begin the next day.

The next morning, at sunrise, "All right, we've got all the savages together, General Scott, sir. Should we begin escorting them to Indian Territory?" asked a lieutenant from the regular U.S. Army.

"The order is given, Lieutenant O'Brian, you may go ahead and carry it out."

"Yes, sir! All right, you savages, get a move on. We ain't got all day! Move!" O'Brian emphasized he was serious by having his men point their Hall breech-loading flintlocks at the Cherokee, which were also equipped with bayonets.

George couldn't see how many Cherokee would be force marched to Indian Territory, but he could tell it was in the hundreds, maybe even thousands. His clan stayed at the back, so he decided to be at the end of the march. This was mostly to watch for people who might collapse from exhaustion so he could help them try to march. The Army followed alongside on their horses and it looked to George that they were amply supplied for this trip, since a supply wagon followed far enough behind that most of the Cherokee wouldn't know it was there. The young Cherokee man begin to feel hatred enter his heart towards these men who were doing this to his people. He knew it was wrong, so he tried praying for peace, but it was a struggle for him not to let the hatred fester in his heart.

As he walked, the air temperature was getting almost cold enough to wear heavier clothes, but he no longer had heavy clothes. George's prayer was that he and everyone else would make it to Indian Territory before the first freeze or first snow fall, whichever came first.

Chapter 2

They were barely sixty miles, three days journey so far, when it began raining, and hard. General Scott's men were pushing the Indians to walk from sunup to sundown, causing some of the elderly to start collapsing to the ground barely two days into the journey. Being at the back, George saw what happened when the older people refused to get up because they were too tired to continue. Some of the soldiers took great delight in bullying the Cherokee, especially when an old person collapsed. From what George could tell, there were at least four bad apples under Scott's command who would poke at the elderly to prod them to get up. If there was no immediate response, the men would begin kicking until there was a response, even if the older person was already dead. In some cases, the men would shoot or impale a body with a bayonet to make sure it was dead. It angered George that General Scott turned a blind eye to the misfortune of the Cherokee.

"All right, all of you get under those trees and get out of the rain. If you're up to it, you can try to scrounge up something to eat, but stay out of land owned by the good folk around here, you might find yourself shot to death. If'n you try to run, you won't get far, 'cause most of the good folk shoot Injuns on sight, especially if you try to go into town. Once it stops raining, we'll continue our march towards Indian Territory." one of the corporals ordered those Cherokee near him.

George helped a couple of his elders to the trees next to the road so they could try to be out of the rain. The trees weren't very protective, since he and everyone else were soaked to the skin, shivering from the cold, and continued to get rained on, but not nearly as much as they would have out in the open. George could hear groaning and crying coming from those ahead of him and then he heard a gunshot in the distance. It sounded like it was somewhere in the trees.

"Stupid savage thought he could get away with stealin' a chicken. Serves him right gettin' shot by that farmer." One of the soldiers said to another as they walked by George in conversation a few minutes later.

"George, do you think we'll be able to make it to Indian Territory?" asked Abigail, his sixty year old aunt, who was shivering and looked a little peaked.

"I hope so, if God is merciful. Are you hungry?"

"Oh, yes, I'm powerful hungry, and so are the others,"

"Maybe I can find a squirrel or something bigger without getting shot,"

"Are you sure? You'd have to capture something with your bare hands, in this cold, wet weather. Maybe you ought to try some other time,"

"Are you sure?"

"I…. I don't know. I want you to, but I also need to feel protected, and you're the only one of us who can do that. Maybe we ought to pray about it. What do you think?"

"I think that's a good idea." George spoke louder so the rest of his clan could hear him, "Everyone, let's gather to pray for guidance so we can have a clear idea what God wants from us,"

When the cold and wet Massey clan gathered around George, he began praying, "Lord in Heaven, we come to you this day in great distress. We're cold, wet, and hungry, so we ask that you direct me to food that I can feed my family with. Please also protect us from the cruelty of these men who are making us march many hundreds of miles across the country to a land unknown to us. Thank you for dying for our sins. Thy will be done, amen."

Not more than five minutes later, a soldier approached the clan, and said to

George, "Ya'll must be really hungry. I've got some hardtack I can give ya'll,"

George was stunned for a moment – this was unexpected. "Thank you, but why?"

"Well, in spite of the fact that I have to take orders and participate in this cruelty, I think this whole escapade will be condemned in the future, and I really want it known for posterity that some of us tried to help. I can't do this very often or for very many, because I'd be punished if I got caught, so here ya go." The soldier handed George ten large pieces of hardtack and then turned around to leave.

"Thank you, sir, may the God of Heaven bless you in all that you do,"

"You're welcome. God bless you too." The unnamed soldier walked away.

"Praise the Lord, we have something to eat."

George set the hardtack on the ground so the rain would soften it up for them to eat. When he began dividing it, he said, "We'll try to stretch how far this lasts, since we don't know when or where our next meal will be. Remember to take your time and don't gulp it down."

The rain ended a couple of hours later and Scott ordered his men to make the Indians start walking again. The road was muddy, making travel slow, but they did their best. Along the way, more Cherokee continued to fall by the wayside, now from a mixture of starvation and exhaustion. Some tried escaping, but sounds of gunfire echoed through the air as the soldiers on horseback chased the fleeing Indians down and shot them. In spite of his best efforts, George couldn't even keep the members of his clan from collapsing to the ground. If he tried to help, the soldiers would force him to keep moving.

Shortly before they neared Nashville two weeks later, someone on horseback approached General Scott, and told him, "Sir, you're to come with me to Nashville. You've been ordered back to Washington,"

"Why?"

"Sorry, sir, I'm not privy to those orders."

"All right, fine. I'll inform my second-in-command that I'll be leaving."

Some of the Cherokee hearing the exchange between the rider and General Scott, stopped walking, even though they weren't supposed to, and caused the others behind them to also stop. Some of them began whispering a rumor that with Scott gone they could stop the march and would be able to go home. They were wrong.

"All right, you lazy savages, stop dilly-dallying and get moving." the nearest soldier ordered.

George's energy levels were falling even though he ate pieces of the hardtack twice a day. He felt he was getting sick, since he wasn't wearing anything that could keep him warm in these November days and the lack of sleep from sleeping on extremely hard ground didn't help matters. He'd lost track of how far they'd traveled, wasn't even sure if they were still in Tennessee or were now in Kentucky, and was getting to the point of being barely aware of anything besides his own problems. The day-in and day-out of almost nonstop walking left him with a dull state of mind. He even stopped paying attention to his own clan and really had no idea he was one of the only ones left.

Being dull of mind finally caught up to George. Snow had been falling for hours and it had already covered the ground, so he wasn't paying attention when he tripped over some other Cherokee who had fallen. George's head hit a rock, which knocked him out. A head wound opened up, enough to have him bleed a little onto the snow.

One of the soldiers saw both bodies as he walked past, and was about to shoot both of them, when another said, "Don't bother.

If they're not dead already, the cold will kill 'em. Let's keep going."

Chapter 3

George woke up.

What he noticed first was being covered in snow, but strangely enough, he really didn't feel very cold. The second thing he noticed was the migraine he now had. He touched his forehead, found the cut, and the large bump surrounding it. It was tender to the touch and painful. Slowly getting up, he saw that the sky was clear of clouds and it was a little bit warmer than it was the last time he was awake.

I wonder how long I've been out? He wondered while he looked around. What he saw saddened him.

There were dozens of dead lining the road, young and old Cherokee alike. The cruelty of humans and what they did to each other continued to amaze George, even though he thought he should be used to the idea by now, but he wasn't. He vowed to himself, *One of these days, I'm going to be rich enough that no one will treat me this way ever again. Even if it takes me the rest of my life.*

With this thought in mind, George realized how cold he really was, so he decided to do something he would never do normally - take the shirts off of the already dead. He found it to be a gruesome task and that most of the clothes were nothing but tatters, but he took what he could. While he went about his task, he prayed, "Lord, please forgive me for this, but I want to live. Please guide me to a place that will accept me for who I am and won't treat me like a savage Indian, but the educated Christian that I am. Thank you, Lord, for getting me this far. In Jesus' name, amen." Then he sat down and cried for a time.

Before he set off to parts unknown, George gathered snow in strips of cloth, wrapped it around his head to try to take the swelling down, and to try to get rid of the pounding headache he had from his head smashing against the rock. Before he could get too far down the road, he heard voices and a horse drawn wagon, so he hid behind some trees to see what the people were doing.

"Let's gather up these bodies so we can bury them in the proper Christian manner. It wouldn't be right for them to just lay here, decaying on the side of the road, where all manner of people can see them. Hurry up now before it gets dark." ordered an older white man to two boys in their teens.

"Yes, sir, Pa, we're getting' right to it."

George watched them for a while, somewhat suspicious of these three's motives. He decided he wouldn't reveal to them he was here, no matter how he felt, because he wasn't sure he could trust them. It didn't matter to him that the three were treating the bodies with care while they loaded them onto the wagon, all George cared about now was survival and avoiding white people altogether. When he was sure they wouldn't see or hear him, he headed off into the woods away from trio.

After spending nearly three exhausting days lost in the woods, George was relieved when he saw a barn in the distance, so he quietly approached it. The house nearby had light streaming from one of its windows and he could barely make out smoke coming from its chimney. Approaching their well, he hoped the owners of this farm wouldn't hear him while he drug up water from the well, drank as much as he could stand, and then slipped into their barn so he could get some rest. Once inside, he saw the ladder to the loft and climbed it while doing his best not to disturb the two horses, the solitary milk cow, and the pigs. The loft had hay all over the floor, so he gathered up what he could, and made a bed to sleep on. He found a blanket stashed in the loft that normally looked like it might be used for the horses, probably when they were saddled. George would use the blanket to keep warm while he slept. Before he went to sleep, George took out the remaining hardtack he still had and ate some. As soon as he laid his head down, he went right to sleep.

The next morning, George was startled awake by a rooster crowing a few feet away from him. It was already daylight and he wondered just how long he'd slept. If it wasn't for the female voice coming from the stall where the milk cow was, George would've hurried as quickly and quietly as he could away from this farm. Now, he felt trapped.

What am I going to do?

He didn't have to wait long for the answer to that question.

"I know someone's up there. I don't know if you're awake, but you should be because the rooster just crowed, most likely near your head. There's also hay on the floor down here where it usually ain't. If you don't speak up, I might have to go get my Pa right after I finish milking Rosie here. My Pa will flush you out with his flintlock and he might take you to the sheriff for trespassing on our land. So, are you gonna come down?"

Feeling like he was in a predicament, George was filled with indecision. He wasn't sure how these people would react to him, especially since he's a Cherokee. Would they shoot him on the spot? Would they really turn him in to the authorities? If he didn't respond to the girl, he knew she would go get her Pa, and George would get shot for trespassing. This felt like a no-win situation. *Lord please help me to do the right thing.*

Deciding to trust in the Lord, George spoke up, but stayed hidden, "I'm sorry about trespassing, but I had nowhere else to go. I saw your barn last night, thought I'd take a few hours to sleep, and then I would slip out of here without any of you knowing I was here. The only thing I was going to do was drink some water from your well before I left. I'm not armed and I mean you no harm,"

"You should be sorry. If my Pa had caught you, there's no telling what he'd do. Come on down here and I'll take you to see my Pa. You ought to know that I've got a pitchfork and I ain't afraid to use it if you try something,"

"All right, I'm coming down."

George slowly got up, feeling sore and still very tired, and made his way down the ladder to the ground. He turned around and faced the young lady. He turned around and saw a bucket of milk on the ground next to her and then he looked at her. He had never been around many whites, so her very red hair startled him, along with her clear blue eyes. She was dressed like every other woman who worked on a farm in this day and age and she was holding the pitchfork like she said she would. To him, she looked to be about sixteen years old.

When she looked at him, all she saw was a man covered in dirt and clothes that were tattered. He had black hair, brown eyes, his complexion, from what she could see through the dirt, was almost brownish, and she thought his tattered clothes vaguely looked like something someone from the Five Civilized Tribes would wear. *Maybe he's Seminole or maybe Choctaw. I guess I'll have to find out.* "Are you from one of those tribes that the government sent to Indian Territory?"

"Yes, I'm Cherokee. I was so hungry and exhausted that I collapsed during the march. I guess they left me for dead, so when I woke up, I wandered around for a couple of days before I found your place. My name's George Massey. By the way, where are we?"

"Nice to meet you, George, I'm Ellie McGregor. You're in Kentucky, near the border with Missouri. So you were on that march west, huh? My Ma and Pa think the government should've left ya'll alone, because they said you weren't doing nothin' but living like you wanted and harmed no one. I'm sorry you had to go through that. Anyway, I better take you to my Pa, he'll know what to do with you. Come on."

Ellie picked up her bucket of milk and continued to hold onto the pitchfork as she pointed George towards the house. On the way there, her ten year old brother appeared, who had the same red hair as his sister, and he excitedly asked, "Is that an Injun?"

"Yes, Jacob, he's from the Cherokee nation and I'm taking him to see Pa. Why don't you go on and keep playing, all right?"

"Oh, all right. See you later, Mr. Injun." Jacob waved at George before he skipped, jumped, and ran out of sight.

"That one's got a lot of energy, never seems to run out if it either, no matter the weather," said Ellie, while George kept walking towards the house in silence.

"Wait here." she said when they came onto the porch, and then she went inside. A couple of rocking chairs sat on the porch, so George sat down in one of them, and waited.

Inside, Ellie found her mother washing clothes, so she asked, "Where's Pa?"

"Oh, he got a visit from Ian McIntosh about helping him bury a bunch of dead

Indians they found down by the road. So that's where he went. What's wrong?"

"I found someone hiding in the barn's loft and he needs help. I thought Pa could help him,"

"Is whoever it is still here? They didn't hurt you did they?"

"Yes, he's still here. No, ma'am, I wasn't hurt. George Massey, which is his name, is on the porch right now. He's been on a long journey and looks cold, hungry, and really tired. Can I bring him in?"

"Of course, since it's our Christian duty to help strangers. Go ahead, bring him in,"

Ellie opened the door and told George he could come in. He could see where Ellie got her looks from, because she was the spitting image of her mother. When George entered, Mrs. McGregor looked somewhat shocked to see that the stranger was an Indian, but had the presence of mind to say, "Welcome to our home, Mr. Massey. So, how did you get to be in the slovenly state you're in?"

"I don't suppose you heard about my people being force marched to Indian Territory, have you?"

"Yes, we have. Nasty business that is, and not very Christian of our so-called self-proclaimed Christian leaders in Washington. How did you manage to get away if you were on that march?"

George retold the same story he told Ellie to Mrs. McGregor. Mrs. McGregor had looks of pity and sadness as George told her the tale, and when he was done, she said, "Well, you're here now, and we'll feed you, clothe you, and give you whatever you need before you decide what to do next. Do you plan on going to Indian Territory once you feel better?"

"I don't know, ma'am. I'm not sure I want to be placed in the same situation again twenty or thirty years from now. I guess I'll go wherever God leads me and if that's where He wants me, then I guess I'll go there."

"I say that's a good Christian attitude to have to let God lead you wherever He wants you. I'll let you speak to my husband when he gets back, he'll help you figure out what to do next. Now, onto more pressing matters, would you like to clean up before we give you something to eat?"

"I would like that very much, ma'am. If I'm not asking for too much, do you have something I could wear too that's not falling apart?"

"Oh, yes, of course. My oldest boys are gone off to live their lives, but they left some clothes behind, we'll see if they fit you. I'll heat up some water for your bath.

For your privacy, we'll put up sheets. Ellie, where's Jacob?"

"He's off playing somewhere,"

"Find him, I want him to help George with towels and his clothes when he's done with the bath. Will you do that, please?"

"Yes, ma'am,"

"Once you find your brother, please get more water from the well so we can give George his bath."

"Yes, ma'am." Ellie left the house in search of Jacob.

While they were waiting, Mrs. McGregor gave George some bread to chew on while waiting for his bath. Then she asked, "So, when did you find out about Christ, George?"

"We had some missionaries from the Methodist church comes to my village when I was ten, which was only ten years ago. They led my whole village to know Christ as their Lord and Savior, then gave the newly established village church to my father, who was also the clan's leader. My father had it until he and my mother died of cholera a few years ago, then I ended up in charge until the Army took us away from there,"

"I'm so sorry, but you'll get to see them in Heaven when you die,"

"I thank God for that every day,"

"Do you have any brothers or sisters?"

"I had a brother, but he tried to stop the militia from burning our homes down. They killed him for it,"

"Again, I'm sorry for your loss, but at least he was a Christian,"

"Yes, ma'am, but that doesn't always make the loss any easier,"

"I understand…."

They were interrupted by Jacob coming through the door, and he said, "Ellie said you needed my help, Ma,"

"Yes, I do. I need you to get some sheets so we can give Mr. Massey some privacy while he's taking a bath, along with a towel so he can dry off. Then, I want you to find some clothes that fits him, probably either from Caleb's or Thomas' remaining clothes. Can you do that for me?"

"Yes, Ma, I'll do that right away!" Jacob bounded off to one of the rooms.

While Jacob brought sheets out, his mother hung them up in a corner of the house where the tub would be. Ellie came in with two buckets of water, poured them into the big pot her mother would use to warm the water, and then she went right out again. The water started getting steaming hot, so with George's help, the two poured the water into the bath. After six times of pouring hot water into the tub, the bath was finally ready.

Chapter 4

The sheets hung from near the ceiling to the floor, so George closed them behind him, and began taking off his dirty, smelly tattered clothes. His new clothes were lying on a chair a few feet away. "What do you want me to do with what's left of my clothes?" he called.

"We'll burn them, since they're too wore out to wear and they smell somethin' awful. Jacob, can you please get them from Mr. Massey." replied Mrs. McGregor.

Jacob reached his hand through the opening in the sheets, since he didn't really want to see George naked. Amused, George placed the clothes in Jacob's hand. It was easy to tell that Jacob had some revulsion to the tattered remains, when he replied, "Yuck!"

"Ellie, would you and Jacob start a fire outside so we can burn these clothes?"

"Yes, Ma." both replied.

George slowly got into the steaming water, which felt good after spending almost three months in the cold, wet weather with mud sticking to him like glue. Before he started using the soap, George soaked in the water for a while. The warm water made his muscles feel better and it relaxed him, almost to the point of wanting to fall asleep. Finally, he cleaned himself off, got out of the tub, dried off, and put on the fresh, new clothes. The clothes were a little big for him, but he was grateful to this family for allowing to get cleaned up and giving him those clothes.

When he stepped out, there was food on the table and the three McGregor's were waiting for him. "I'm sure you're famished, George, so lunch is on the table," said Ellie.

"I sure am." He replied while sitting down. "So, what's for lunch?"

"Chicken fried steak, mashed potatoes, corn, and bread, along with fresh milk," replied Mrs. McGregor.

"One of my favorite meals. I'm sure I'll enjoy every morsel, ma'am,"

"Would you like to say grace, George?"

"All right." Everyone bowed their heads, as George began, "Dear Heavenly Father, we thank you this day for this meal we're about to receive. Thank you for guiding me to this family and thank you for their hospitality. Please continue to lead, guide, and direct us in the way we should go. In your name, amen."

While they were eating, Ellie noticed the still rather large, slightly black and blue, bump on George's head, since his being covered in mud and dirt hid it before. "Does that hurt?"

"Not as much as it did, but it's still tender to the touch. I had a bad headache when I woke up after I hit a rock, but it's pretty much gone now. I can even see straight again,"

"That's good. We've known people who've hit their heads and were never the same again. I'm glad you still feel like yourself."

Thanks, Ellie."

The four ate their meal and George enjoyed it. He still wasn't sure he trusted this family, but they seemed like good Christian folk. He was debating within himself when he should leave for Indian Territory, mostly because he wanted to find out what happened to the rest of his clan, but this being winter, he thought it would probably be best to wait for spring. Although, he wasn't sure the McGregor's would tolerate him as a guest for that long. When they finished the meal, he helped the McGregor's clean up the dishes.

Before they settled down, Jacob said, "I think I hear a wagon coming. Maybe Pa's comin' home. I'll go out and look!" The boy pulled open the door and looked outside, turned around to look at everyone else. "It is

Pa! Mr. McIntosh is bringing him back. I'll go get him."

"Is he always so full of energy?" asked George.

"He has more energy than my three other children combined. I hope and pray he goes through life with boundless energy and that nothing will get him down. George, you stay here while I go tell him we have a visitor, all right?" replied Mrs. McGregor.

"All right."

"Coming, Ellie?"

"I'll be right there, Ma." Ellie replied, while putting the remaining clean dishes in the cupboard.

Outside, Jacob greeted his father as he was stepping off of the wagon, "Hi, Pa. We've got a visitor,"

Before replying to his son, he said to McIntosh, "Thank you for bringing me back, Ian. If ya'll want more help, you know where to find me. Have safe trip back."

"You're welcome, Duncan. See you later." McIntosh tipped his hat, prompted his horses to start, and they headed back the way they came.

"Hey there, Jacob. We have a visitor? Who is it?"

Before Jacob could reply, Mrs. McGregor said after kissing her husband, and began walking hand-in-hand together towards the house, "Welcome home, husband. Yes, we have a visitor. He's one of the poor souls that the government pushed out of their lands. He found himself lost and ended up here. We cleaned him up and fed him,"

"An Indian? What tribe does he claim, Moira?"

"He's Cherokee,"

"Hi, Pa," Ellie said when she walked up to them and kissed her father on the cheek.

"Good afternoon, my only daughter." He kissed her on the forehead and then turned back to his wife, "Ah. We just buried a few hundred of 'em that were laying out on the main road. Pitiful sight, that was. He tell how he escaped?"

"Yes, he's inside the house. You don't mind, do you?"

"No, of course I don't. Well, we'll go inside and I'll have a talk with him and see what he wants to do next. By the way, I have a letter from Caleb."

"I'm so glad. We'll read it together later and find out what he's up to in Texas."

George felt nervous about meeting Mr. McGregor, mostly because he didn't know how the man would react to him. He thought whites seemed like overly complicated people and one could never tell how honest and straight forward they would be, but that was based on his limited experience around them. The door opened and Mr. McGregor entered with his family surrounding him.

George saw that the man was tall, around six feet, built like he could chop down a really big tree without any help, and also had red hair. George stood up, offered his hand, and said, "Hello, I'm George Massey,"

McGregor took George's hand and shook it, although the Cherokee young man felt like the older man could break the bones in his hand without really trying. "Hello, Mr. Massey, I'm Duncan McGregor, head of this house. I understand you were part of the group that the U.S. Army was escorting to Indian Territory,"

"Yes, sir,"

"How'd you manage to get away from them?"

George retold his story to the older man. Duncan listened to the whole story and said, "I'm sure you wonder why we're not calling for the sheriff or the Army to come get you. Right?"

"The thought did cross my mind,"

"There's a very good reason why we wouldn't do such a thing. My ancestors in Scotland fought England centuries ago, similar to how some of the Indian tribes here are, so England over-reacted by sending a bunch of the so-called troublemakers by force to Ireland. There they stayed until a group of them, including my parents and Moira's, decided to leave and come to this country after the War for Independence. They settled here in Kentucky and decided not to turn away anyone who needed help, because we feel we share similar histories. It doesn't matter if they were Indians or escaped slaves, all was welcome in our community. You're welcome to stay, but that's really up to you,"

"Thank you for the offer and to be honest, I'm not sure what to do next,"

"I have an idea. My two oldest sons used to help me with the plowing of our land when we plant in the spring, plus the chopping of wood, hunting for meat, but they're no longer here, since they're off living their lives. Jacob's too young to help right now when it comes to man-sized work and Ellie's got her own chores to do, so would you consider working for me? You'll have free room and board, along with getting to eat some excellent food cooked by Moira and Ellie,"

"I'll consider it, sir, but I also have to eventually go to Indian Territory to find out if any of my clan made it there. I'm sure you understand,"

"Yes, I understand. You need to do what's best for you, although I would suggest waiting 'til late spring, early summer before you go west,"

"I think that's a good idea, sir."

"Good, we've got that settled. Now, would ya'll like to hear what Caleb has to say in his latest letter?"

The family replied they wanted to hear it, but Duncan decided to tell George a little about Caleb, "Before I begin, George, you ought to know that Caleb is in Texas. He helped fight for their independence from Mexico and now lives in San Antonio with his new wife, Sarah,"

"Fighting against Santa Anna must've been a harrowing experience,"

"We tried talkin' him out of if, but he wanted adventure, and so he got it. Sam Houston himself, or so Caleb claims, parceled out fifty acres of land to Caleb for helpin' the Texians defeat Mexico,"

"Your son must've been grateful for that. Does he know if Texas will ever become a part of these United States?"

"He actually mentions that in this letter, so I'll go ahead and read it aloud.

Dear Family,
I hope all is well with you
and that this letter finds you
in good health. Sarah and I

are fine and we have some good news – Sarah's expecting our first child. We're not sure when he or she will be born, but we expect sometime around summer. Tell Ma that Sarah's own Ma is helping out and there's no need to worry.

I'm sure you're wondering about the state of affairs in these parts. Well, the debate's been raging about if Texas will ever join the Union. Some want it, others think Texas ought to stay a Republic. In order to pay for the debts, Texas sells its lands to people like myself or to men who would like to do some ranching or farming. It's all very exciting.

I hope we can see each other either again sometime and I love all of you. May God bless everything our family does and all of you continue to follow what God wants from you.

Your loving son and brother, Caleb."

"He didn't say much, did he?" replied Moira.

"Caleb never was one for long letters, I'm just glad he writes us anything. So, George, do you have anyone you want to write to?"

"No, sir. While the missionaries taught us to read the Bible, they didn't teach us our letters, so I couldn't write anyone even if I did have someone to write to. Because the soldiers kicked me out of my home and burned it down, I don't even have a Bible to read,"

"I'm sorry, George. We'll give you a Bible for you to use that you won't have to give back. Moira can help you with your letters, because she was a schoolteacher for a short time before we were married and she taught our first two children when there was no school around these parts. If you're willing, that is,"

"I would like that and I'd like to learn to read more than just the Bible, because I have a hard time reading anything else. Would you mind, Mrs. McGregor?"

"I wouldn't mind at all, George, it would be my pleasure. Since there's very little work to do during the winter, we can take some time before March comes to teach you a little bit, all right?"

"That'll be fine with me. Thank you, ma'am."

For the rest of the day, the whole family worked with George on his letters and showed him some other written works that he could us to practice his reading. When night fell, Duncan took out his bagpipes, which was something George had never seen or heard before, and began playing songs on it, while his family either listened or danced to. When they went to bed, he slept in the same room as Jacob, since there was an extra bed. The Cherokee young man felt at home with this family, no matter how odd they seemed to him, and he continued to wonder if everyone in this community was as open-minded as the McGregor's. George figured he would soon find out.

Chapter 5

Sunday came around and the family prepared to go to church. George was looking forward to going and was glad he didn't have to sermonize to anyone. When he led his people at his home church, George mostly read a chapter from the Bible and tried his best to explain what it meant. He knew God would speak to the hearts and minds of the people, no matter how much he stumbled and stuttered when trying to preach a sermon. His father tried to imitate Mr. Massey, the missionary, but he wasn't too good at it either. Now, with his new Bible, even though it was one of many owned by the McGregor's, George looked forward to hearing sermons preached by a real preacher. The McGregor's and George piled into the wagon, dressed in their Sunday best, and started off for church, which was a little over an hour away from the McGregor's home. The weather was warmer than it had been, so there was no need to be dressed in their winter clothes. Moira and Ellie pre-prepared a picnic lunch and put it in the wagon.

The church was painted white and was on the edge of a town called Paducah.

George was told by the McGregor's that Paducah was on the Kentucky border with the Ohio River, with the state of Missouri on the other side of the river. The history of the place as told to him was that Paducah was laid out in 1827 by William Clark, of the Lewis and Clark Expedition. The town was officially established in 1830, then became incorporated a few months before George's arrival. This was in spite of the fact that settlers had stopped here in 1815 and had named their community Pekin. In 1827, The Supreme Court of the United States had given Clark the title of the land and he reorganized the town and everyone's property. Because of the town's location, steamboat companies began using Paducah as a port facility and a lot of trade occurred in the town.

The wagon was stopped where the other horses and wagons were and the family got off the wagon. The pastor of the church was outside greeting everyone as they went in. Duncan shook the man's hand, and said to him, "Pastor Bowen, this is George Massey, he'll be visiting with us for a while,"

"It's nice to meet you. Where do you come from?"

George hesitated to tell him, since one never knew how others would react to hearing that he was a Cherokee. Sighing, he replied, "I'm from northwestern Georgia. I happen to be Cherokee and found myself here because the United States forced my people on a march west,"

"Oh…."

"George is welcome here, isn't he, Pastor?" asked Duncan, who could see Pastor Bowen was trying to think of what to do next.

"Oh, um, of course he is. Go right on in."

Inside, the pews were filling up and the McGregor's went to sit in their usual spot three rows from the back. Before George made it too far, one man came up to him, and said, "Shouldn't you be with your people and those supposedly freed Negroes at their church?"

"Sorry, what?"

"You heard me, savage,"

"Who are you?" asked Duncan, who put himself between George and the man he didn't know.

"Me? I'm just a concerned citizen who doesn't want to mix with the likes of this dirty savage,"

"You must be new here then, because we in here in Paducah have blacks and Indians living here too. Peacefully, I might add, because of the river trade. Why don't you leave George alone and be more Christ-like?

The man's face got red with anger, "You want us to leave him alone? Fine. Martha, gather up our children, because we're leaving. Anyone that mixes with savages and darkies are obviously wrong in the head. Besides, there's more than one church in this town we can go to where only the pure folk are. Goodbye."

The man, his wife, and their dozen children left the church, with all eyes from the church members on George, making him feel really uncomfortable. He sat down next to Duncan, but people in the pews in front of them got up and moved to other pews. However, no one else left the church. Duncan rolled his eyes and said to George, "Don't worry about them folks, they'll have to answer to God in eternity for their treatment of you and others like you. Pastor Bowen said it was all right for you be here, so don't worry on it. All right?"

"I'll try not to, Mr. McGregor."

Everything settled down once the services began, everyone sang hymns, and then Pastor Bowen walked up to his podium to start preaching. "Our message today is about Nicodemus and his questions about how one can be born again. Please open your Bibles to John 3, and we'll read from verses one to twenty-one.

[1]There was a man of the Pharisees, named Nicodemus, a ruler of the Jews:

[2] The same came to Jesus by night, and said unto him, Rabbi, we know that thou art a teacher come from God: for no man can do these miracles that thou doest, except God be with him.

[3] Jesus answered and said unto him, Verily, verily, I say unto thee, Except a man be born again, he cannot see the kingdom of God.

[4] Nicodemus saith unto him, How can a man be born when he is old? can he enter the second time into his mother's womb, and be born?

[5] Jesus answered, Verily, verily, I say unto thee, Except a man be born of water and of the Spirit, he cannot enter into the kingdom of God.

[6] That which is born of the flesh is flesh; and that which is born of the Spirit is spirit.

⁷ Marvel not that I said unto thee, Ye must be born again.

⁸ The wind bloweth where it listeth, and thou hearest the sound thereof, but canst not tell whence it cometh, and whither it goeth: so is every one that is born of the Spirit.

⁹ Nicodemus answered and said unto him, How can these things be?

¹⁰ Jesus answered and said unto him, Art thou a master of Israel, and knowest not these things?

¹¹ Verily, verily, I say unto thee, We speak that we do know, and testify that we have seen; and ye receive not our witness.

¹² If I have told you earthly things, and ye believe not, how shall ye believe, if I tell you of heavenly things?

¹³ And no man hath ascended up to heaven, but he that came down from heaven, even the Son of man which is in heaven.

¹⁴ And as Moses lifted up the serpent in the wilderness, even so must the Son of man be lifted up:

¹⁵ That whosoever believeth in him should not perish, but have eternal life.

¹⁶ For God so loved the world, that he gave his only begotten Son, that whosoever believeth in him should not perish, but have everlasting life.

¹⁷ For God sent not his Son into the world to condemn the world; but that the world through him might be saved.

¹⁸ He that belicvcth on him is not condemned: but he that believeth not is condemned already, because he hath not believed in the name of the only begotten Son of God.

¹⁹ And this is the condemnation, that light is come into the world, and men loved darkness rather than light, because their deeds were evil.

20 For every one that
doeth evil hateth the light,
neither cometh to the light,
lest his deeds should be
reproved.
21 But he that doeth truth
cometh to the light, that his
deeds may be made manifest,
that they are wrought in God.

"Now, as you can see by what Christ told Nicodemus after his many questions, the only way to enter the Kingdom of Heaven is to accept that Jesus is our Savior. You must accept Him into your life so you can be saved from the fires of Hell. You must also be baptized after you receive Jesus because it shows publicly that you've made a confession of faith. No man or woman can save themselves, you must be born again through the flesh and spirit, so you too can become new men and women through Christ. I know many of you are going to Heaven, but some of you are not, so as I close, please come to the altar during the invitation so we can help you accept Christ into your life. Now I'll pray."

The invitation was given after the sermon, and George saw that a dozen people had gone to the altar to seek Christ. The church elders, he guessed they were, helped the lost people accept Christ as their Savior by praying with them. Once that was done, the dozen stood at the front so everyone in the congregation could shake their hands, and nearly everyone in the congregation did so.

Once the McGregor's and George got the wagon, Moira asked, "Where should we go for a picnic?"

"We could always picnic next to the river. What do you think?" Duncan suggested.

"Can we, Ma?" asked Ellie.

"All right, we can do that. Do you have your fishing rod, Dear?"

"Of course. I brought three, since Jacob always goes fishing with me, and so George can too. How about it George, want to go fishing?" Duncan asked, while putting his arm around George's shoulder.

"Sure, I haven't gone fishing in a long time."

"Good, sounds like we have a plan. Let's go."

The five found the spot near the river where the McGregor's usually picnicked. The river was too cold to swim in, but Duncan, George, and Jacob had no problem catching fish. Moira and Ellie prepared the rest of the food and laid out the blanket on the ground that they'd be sitting and eating on. It only took the men two hours to catch six fish and that's what they ate for lunch, along with side dishes. An hour and half before sunset, they cleaned up the site, and went home.

Chapter 6

Weeks later, George was becoming acclimated to living with the McGregor's, even though he knew he should set out one day to Indian Territory to find out what happened to his clan. It was now spring, so it was getting warm enough to work outside on a regular basis. Moira and Ellie worked on a little garden close to the house, which would be full of tomatoes, melons, beans, lettuce, and squash, while the main crop on their lands that Duncan usually planted was corn.

"My corn is one of the best around these parts, George. The freight companies buy a great deal from me around harvest time and I make enough money to last until the next harvest. We're always careful not to spend too much, because you always have to be prepared for a season where there might be a sudden depression, which causes the value of various things to plummet, including food. Then there's hail, drought, grasshoppers, along with any number of other crop killing disasters. I've seen a few of those in my lifetime, and I pray I don't see any more,"

"What do you need me to do, sir?"

"George, quit calling me sir, all right? I would prefer if you would call me Duncan. There's no need for formalities between us. I'm just a farmer, not landed gentry,"

"I'll do that, uh, Duncan,"

"Now that we've got that out of the way - do you know how to hook up the plow to one of the horses? And, do you know how to steer the horse as you plow the land?"

"No, my clan didn't have the equipment you do, Mr. McGregor. We had to do everything by hand, so our crops were much smaller,"

"I see. Well, my boy, it'll be easy to learn. Go fetch Jacob, he should be taking care of the animals, and he'll show you what to do. I'm going to clear another one or two acres, so that's what I'll be doing while you plow. My other son, Thomas, usually helps me. He owns a store in Paducah, so all he has to do is have his wife run the store while he's helping me. Think you can handle plowing at least some of the five acres for me?"

"I think so."

"Good. Now, let's get to work."

George found Jacob, who was cleaning out the chicken coop and replacing the old hay with new hay. "Jacob, I'm going to need your help,"

"With what?"

"Your Pa wants me to plow, but I've never actually hooked up a plow to a horse before, so he said I should ask you for help,"

"I'm almost done with this, can you wait?"

"I suppose. Do you want any help?"

"Naw, I'll be done in a minute. After I help you though, I've gotta put more water in the barrel they drink from, 'cause they're almost out."

Jacob finished mucking out the coop and laying the fresh hay. To George, the chickens seemed to be pleased, as they clucked and pecked at the new hay. Jacob led George to the barn, where one horse remained, since the other one was with Duncan, and would be used to pull small tree stumps and haul rocks away. Jacob pulled out the plow, which looked new to George, and he pointed it out.

"Yup, it's new. The last one Pa used for years got all rusty and fell apart. This one is supposed to be the latest in farming, according to Pa, who says he heard it through word of mouth. It's made by a blacksmith in Illinois by the name of John Deere. It's not supposed to clog as you're tilling, I guess because of the blade being steel instead of cast-iron. Anyway, after I put the tack on Hank, I'll hook the plow up to him and I'll help you lead him to the plot you're supposed to plow."

"Thanks for your help, Jacob."

Once they were where George was supposed to plow, Jacob said, "Our horses have been doing this for years, they know what they're doing, so don't worry about staying in a straight line. Just say 'giddy up' and Hank will go. When you get to the end of the first row, Hank will turn and you'll till the second row, then the third, up until you're done. When you feel you're done, just tell him 'woah' and Hank will stop. Got it?"

"Yeah. Um, what about when I get thirsty or hungry?"

"Oh, I think Ma or Ellie is gonna take care of that,"

"I hope so. How long do you think it'll take me to plow what your Pa wants me to plow?"

"Usually, it takes him a week, sometimes two, to plow five acres,"

George's jaw dropped, "Really?"

"Yup, but at least you don't have to plow hundreds of acres. Pa says for that to happen, he'd need hired hands or slaves. He doesn't believe in slavery and he says it would be too expensive to hire men to help him, so he does what he can. I better get back to my chores, see you later."

Sighing, George grabbed the reins and loosely wrapped them around the handles of the plow. "Well, here goes nothing. Hank, giddy up."

George was startled when the horse started off faster than he'd anticipated and he almost lost his balance. After a few minutes of guiding the plow, George was glad he was wearing a hat because the sun felt hot to him, but he wished he had a bucket of water near him so he could stop to take a break. *I wonder why I decided to wait for someone to bring me water? Boy, am I stupid.*

Not really noticing how much time had passed, George's focus on plowing was interrupted when he heard someone shouting at him. "Woah, Hank," George ordered the horse and then looked towards where the voice was coming from. Looking across the plowed up field, George hadn't realized he had done a lot already, but now he was more focused on the person calling to him. He thought the woman calling him and waving at him was Ellie, but he wasn't sure, since she was wearing a bonnet. It was obvious to him that she had brought him water, so he got out from behind the plow and made his way to where she was standing.

"Hey, George, it's time for lunch. You and Hank must be really thirsty, since I don't see any water out here,"

"Hi, Ellie. Yeah, I didn't think of it until I started plowing, and that was really dumb of me. Thank you for bringing it. I think that's sweet of you,"

Ellie blushed, but George was hot and thought she was too, since he wasn't very familiar with womanly ways. "Oh, I wanted to do it. I also brought you lunch. We can eat lunch together, if you'd like,"

"I would be honored,"

Ellie laid out the blanket and the food on plates. George sat down, took off his sweat soaked hat, and asked, "So, what's for lunch?"

"I've got chicken, zucchini bread, and an apple pie for dessert,"

"Sounds good, let's eat."

After they ate the main lunch and before dessert, George brought the water to the horse and made sure Hank had cooled down before letting the horse drink so he wouldn't get colic later. Hank drank a lot of it and then patiently stood where he was when George went back to Ellie so they could finish off the apple pie.

While the two were eating, Moira and Jacob took some food to Duncan and

Thomas. While they were setting out the food, Duncan asked, "Where's Ellie?"

"She fixed lunch for George and they're eating together,"

"Oh, I see,"

"What do you mean by that, husband?"

"What do I mean by what?" he asked, with a hint of amusement in his eyes.

"Come now, you know very well what I'm asking. What do you mean by 'Oh, I see?' I suspect I know why, but I still want to hear your explanation," Moira crossed her arms across her chest.

"I'm thinking our little Ellie is sweet on George, while George seems oblivious to the whole matter,"

"I think so too, she talks about him a lot, especially when we were gardening earlier. George, on the other hand, looks like he's overwhelmed being here, and is too distracted to notice how much she likes him,"

"I think I ought to talk to him, to see how he feels about her, and discuss with him how hard it might be for the two of them if they both feel the same way. I'll talk with him after supper, all right?"

"Thank you, my husband. I won't worry so much about either of them if you clear the air with George. Now, are you hungry?"

"Famished, my dear."

Later in the day, after the work of the day was done and everyone was finished with their dinner, Duncan asked George to go outside with him so they could talk. Once they were on the porch, both sat down on rocking chairs, and then George asked, "What do you want to talk to me about?"

"One of the things I was wanting to know was what your plans were for the next couple of months. Have you decided on anything?"

"I think I'll go to Indian Territory after I help you plow and seed. Mostly, I just want to see what happened to my clan, and not just the ones who were force marched there, but the ones who left years earlier on their own,"

"I understand, you need to do what you need to do. You know we'll miss you, including Ellie, who seems to have become fond of you. Have you noticed?"

"I'll miss you too. As for Ellie, I'm unfamiliar with the ways of the whites when it comes to matters between men and women. In my culture, marriages were arranged when we were very young by the parents and they had to be of different clans. The boy and girl had no say in the matter, and when we were of the appropriate age, we consummated the marriage,"

"Ah, it was the same in the old world with my culture. Moira and I were betrothed to each other when we were small. We've been lucky that we actually liked each other as we grew, enjoyed courting each other, but we have known others who were – what's a good word?" Duncan took the time to think of the appropriate word before he said, "Mismatched. Yes, that's what they were, although a bit of an understatement if I do say so. Moira and I pledged to let our children choose their own mates without interference from us, since we're in a new country where such a thing is allowed. If you like Ellie, her mother and I wouldn't stand in your way if you want to court her,"

"I appreciate that, Duncan, but I hadn't really thought about her in that way. No offense is intended,"

"None taken, George, so please speak your mind,"

"You see, I also plan on finding out if the girl I was intended for is still alive and if she still plans on honoring the commitment our parents made for us. If she does, then I'll do what I must, what my culture demands of me. However, if things have changed, I might consider Ellie as someone I could, how you say, court. I'm honored that Ellie considers me as someone who she'd like as a suitor, but as I said, it's just not possible right now. I hope you understand,"

"Yes, I do understand. Thank you for being honest with me. One last thing, you do know some people will object to you and Ellie, if such an arrangement did happen, don't you?"

"Yes, I'm aware of the problem, but I think we ought to cross that river when we get to it."

"I agree. Now, let's go in and get warm."

After the McGregor's and George spent the next month and a half clearing the land and then seeding it, George began to feel like he should leave, but he wasn't sure exactly how he would get to Indian Territory. One thing he did know, God would provide the means when the time came and he would wait until the door was open to him.

Chapter 7

The door to go to Indian Territory opened for George less than two weeks later in the first week of April. An Irish born freight trader, by the name of Seamus O'Hara, traveling on the Ohio River drifted in on a large raft into Paducah with his wares. He sold items the larger steamboat companies didn't sell, so the townsfolk, including the McGregor's, went to see what he was selling. While he described his wares to the eager people, someone asked him about where he was going to next, "I'm makin' my way towards Fort Smith, that's in Arkansas, on the border with Indian Territory. Them in the Army is watchin' them Indians they brought up from Georgia and Tennessee, so I'm figurin' they's gonna need some of the stuff I'm sellin' for their womenfolk. Them Indians probably need some stuff too, if they've got themselves some money to do some tradin' with me. I'm only gonna be 'round these parts 'til daybreak tomorrow, so get what you need now."

The McGregor's bought what they needed and were about to leave, when George stood where he was. Duncan said,

"We're headed back home, George, are you coming?"

"I think I'll wait to speak to the man about me going along with him. It shouldn't be very long before everyone in town are done doing business with him,"

"If that's what you want to do, we won't get in your way. Be careful, though, you might find yourself sold down the river as someone's slave,"

"I understand. Don't worry about me, I'll return to the house when I'm done speaking with him,"

"All right. We'll pray for God to show you the way and for Him to protect you. We'll be on our way now." The family waved at George as they left the docks.

George waited for two hours before the townsfolk finally dispersed and he approached the raft. O'Hara was adding up his transactions, when George said, "Hello there, can I speak with you?"

The trader was startled by the interruption, but turned around, scowled, and asked, "Who might you be?"

"My name's George Massey. I heard you were headed for Fort Smith next. I was wondering if I could go with you?"

"I don't want no partner, I's perfectly fine by me self,"

"I'm not asking to partner with you, Mr. O'Hara, I plan on getting off at Fort Smith. I can feed myself and I'll stay out of your way. You'll barely know I'm there,"

O'Hara scratched at his beard, "I don't know...."

"Is it because I'm an Indian?"

"No, no, that ain't me reasoning. You never know who's gonna rob you blind...."

"If you need someone to vouch for me, I have people you can talk to," interrupted George.

"You're a persistent cuss, ain't ya? Fine, let me get me stuff tied down and secured, and we'll go speak with whoever you want me to speak with. Is that all right with you?"

"Yes, sir. I can wait."

A short time later, both men came to the McGregor's. O'Hara grumbled the entire way about having to deal with unreasonable people. Duncan was putting up the horses, when George approached him, introduced the two men to each other, and said, "Mr. O'Hara wants you to vouch for me before he lets me go along with him,"

"Ah, no problem there. George is a fine, trustworthy Christian young man. He's lived with us now for a couple of months and he's been a great help to us with plowing, seeding, and various other chores. You needn't worry about him,"

"All right, fine, he gets to come with me. If you cause me trouble, off you go, and you'd be left to your own devices. Also, be at the raft at the sun's risin' or you'll be left behind. Do we have an understandin'?"

"Yes, sir." Both men shook hands.

"So, Mr. O'Hara, what part of Ireland do you claim?" asked Duncan, while finishing up with the horses.

"I come from County Dublin. I heard America was a land where you could write your own destiny, so here I be. Where do you hail from, McGregor?"

"My family were Ulster Scots, my family came to this great land a little later than everyone else from Ulster,"

"Yeah, Ulster does seem to be emptying out, but I don't think the English will ever give it back to the Irish," interrupted O'Hara, who spat on the ground when he mentioned England.

"Well, uh, we too enjoy the freedom we have to do whatever we want. But, that's enough talk about the old world. O'Hara, do you have any plans for supper?"

"No, I's usually on me own,"

"How would you like to share our food with us? You're welcome to stay for supper,"

"If it ain't too much trouble for the missus,"

"No, no trouble at all. Come, let me introduce you to the rest of the family."

O'Hara felt better about his decision once he met the rest of the McGregor's and had supper with them, but he was still wary about taking on passengers. *As long as hitchin' a ride don't become a regular event with other folks, George is welcome on me raft, as long as he don't take advantage of the situation.* O'Hara thought to himself before praying, *Lord, please keep us safe on the journey and please help George find who he's looking for in Indian Territory. Please also give me the wisdom to do the right thing. In your name, I pray, amen."*

Before George left the McGregor's the next morning before sunrise, the family took the time to wish him goodbye. "I hope you find what you're looking for and God protects you on your journey." said Duncan.

"I prepared some meals for you, including some hardtack, and put it in this pail, that way you don't have to rely on Mr. O'Hara. We'll miss you." Moira handed George a large pail full of food.

"I want to thank all of you for the kindness you showed me these last few months, it was something most wouldn't do if an Indian showed up at their door. I won't forget it. I pray that God blesses your family in everything you do,"

"You won't forget to write us if you get the chance?" asked Ellie, who was on the verge of tears.

"I will when I get an opportunity. Who knows, maybe I'll end up coming back here, so please don't act like this'll be last time we see each other, all right?"

"All right." Then, out of the blue, she gave George an unexpected hug and ran back into the house. George wasn't sure how to react, but did feel a little sorry that he was leaving.

"Thank you for fishing and goin' frogging with me, George." said Jacob.

"Oh, you're welcome. I had fun. Well, I best get along, don't want Mr. O'Hara to leave without me. Bye." George shook their hands and the McGregor's waved while he walked towards town.

Just before the sun peaked over the horizon, George came onto the raft as O'Hara prepared to disembark from the pier his raft was tied to. "About time you got here, the sun's about to rise. I thought you got lost or something,"

"No, just saying my goodbyes to the McGregor's,"

"They seems like nice folk. Not many are these days. Do you expect to see them again?"

"I can't say, only God really knows the future, but I think I'd like to one day. Anyway, how long will it take us to get to Fort Smith?"

"At most, it'll take three weeks, seeing as to how I have wares that the good folk need who live off the Mississippi and Arkansas rivers. Not many towns betwixt here and Fort Smith, but I'm willing to bet that changes in the next few years. Even them Indians in the territory could use some of my wares. What do you think?"

"Wouldn't hurt to find out. Do you go any further than Fort Smith or Indian Territory?"

"Nope, after I visit the fort, I return home to South Carolina, where I get me wares. By the time I get there, it'll be close to fall, so no selling on the rivers during the wintertime. Once spring arrives, I do this all over again. I enjoy me freedom, no government telling me what I can or can't do. I gets to live life the way I want. All right, time to shove off."

O'Hara untied the rope to the pier and pushed away using one of the poles he used to guide the raft along the river. The two men then began the journey towards Fort Smith by first going down the Ohio, followed by a short journey down the Mississippi, and then onto the Arkansas

River, which would go right past the Army
fort, where they would stop.

Chapter 8

Over the next three weeks, O'Hara stopped the raft at small settlements next to one of the three rivers so the settlers could have a chance to look at his wares. He told George that he hoped most of them had cash money because he disliked being paid with livestock or produce, since those were hard to resell as most everyone in these parts grew or raised the same things. George mostly stayed out of sight and usually went fishing or hunting in nearby woods, mostly to keep himself occupied, and if he wanted something different to eat than what Moira had packed for him.

Traveling with the Irishman was intcresting for George, because the older man told him stories about Ireland, including some of the tall tales. "Have you heard about leprechauns?"

"What are they?"

With a twinkle in his eyes, O'Hara smiled and replied, "Leprechauns are wee fairy folk, usually seen as an old man, standing almost to me knees, and are shoe makers. Depending on where someone lives in Ireland, the wee fairies wear red or green coats. They also cause a whole lot of mischief. I'm sure you've seen rainbows?"

"What are rainbows?" George hadn't heard the English term before.

"You know, it's that band of colors in the sky after it rains,"

"Oh, I do know it. In the Tsalagi language, which is Cherokee to you, a rainbow is called 'unvquolada.' Most whites have a hard time hearing the subtleties of my language, so I don't usually say anything in Tsalagi. What do these leprechauns have to do with rainbows?"

"These wee folk store all of their gold coins at the end of a rainbow in a hidden pot. If one of us humans manage to capture one, they'll grant three wishes so the human will release them. Not one soul I know has managed to catch one, because rainbows disappear so quickly,"

"Can you find leprechauns here?"

"Nay, only in Ireland," O'Hara had a hard time keeping a straight face.

"Have you seen one though?"

O'Hara couldn't hold back his laughter.

"Were you fooling me?"

"Aye, very few people fall for it, but you did. Thanks for the laugh, George. The leprechaun is a very ancient part of Irish folklore. I would think you have similar tall tales in your culture,"

"Yes, I think we do have something very similar in my people's stories. We have a story about the trickster named Jistu, which in your language is known as the rabbit. He plays nasty tricks on the other animals. He's also a glutton, careless, and has an overinflated ego. According to the legends of my people, he also stole fire and brought it to us when the people were hungry and cold. I have more stories about Jistu, and other legends of my people, if you'd like to hear them."

"Aye, I would. I'll tell you more of mine too, since we still have a ways to go."

A few days later, they found themselves approaching Fort Smith. The fort itself had a partial stone wall that looked to be in the middle of being built around the fort and O'Hara said it was the second version of the original fort, since they could also see new buildings in the fort's perimeter. The original Fort Smith was founded in 1817, but abandoned in 1824 when the Army moved operations to Fort Gibson in Indian Territory. However, with the Indian Removal Act of 1830, the federal government decided to reopen the fort so they could have an even stronger military presence in the west.

Outside of the fort, the town was increasing in size. A few dozen buildings were in various stages of construction, from partial and fully framed skeletons to a handful of complete structures. A small port and trading post had been already built, so O'Hara directed the raft towards one of the piers and tied the raft's rope to the pier.

"George, I'll be here until me raft's almost completely empty, not more than a week I reckon, so if you need to return east, you have that long to find out if you stay or go. All right?"

"I understand. Thank you for allowing me to travel with you, Mr. O'Hara."

"It was a pleasure, George." They shook hands and George walked away.

George made his way towards the fort. Two enlisted men were guarding each side of the entrance, so he asked one of them, "I was wondering if the Army keeps records here about the Cherokee who made their way into Indian Territory?"

"Yes, the Army keeps records, but at Fort Gibson, in Indian Territory, where the Indians are," answered the corporal to his left with a hint of sarcasm.

"How far would that be?"

"It's probably about seventy, maybe eighty miles, about a day and a half walk from here. You just follow the Arkansas River until it splits with the Canadian, continue to go north along the Arkansas for a little ways, and there you'll find Fort Gibson." replied the corporal on George's right.

"Thank you for your help." George sighed. He felt a little bit disappointed that he'd have to go somewhere else to find out if anyone in his clan still lived and if his betrothed still wanted him. He never considered giving up, especially since he'd gotten this far, so another seventy miles didn't give him pause. Before he did anything else, George decided he needed to send a letter back to the McGregor's, so he went to the Post Office, asked for a pencil and paper, and began his letter.

> To the McGregor's,
> I hope this letter finds all of you in good health. I finally made it to Fort Smith and I'm still in good health. Mr. O'Hara was an interesting travel companion and I learned a lot about Ireland and its history. At Fort Smith, I found out that I need to travel to an Army fort in Indian Territory to locate the people I'm looking for, so that's where I'm headed to next. I pray that my journey hasn't been for naught.

I close this letter by saying
that I continue to be grateful
for everything you did for me
and I thank God continuously
you were there for me. I pray
that God keeps your family in
good health for the rest of
your natural lives.
Your Friend,
George Massey.

George folded the letter into an envelope, sealed it, and paid for the postage. The postal clerk informed him it would take around a month for the letter to reach Paducah, which George was fine with, since it was normal for communications to be so slow. Once he was finished, George walked away and continued on his journey.

George had enough food and had no problem sleeping under the stars, so the trip didn't worry him. As he walked, he prayed, *Heavenly Father, thank you for getting me this far. Please give me the wisdom to do what I need to do and please help me to find everyone I need to find. If I'm not supposed to be here, then please make it known to me that the door is firmly closed. Thank you for everything you do for me. In Jesus' name, amen.*

A day and a half later, George found himself in front of what looked like a heavily fortified U.S. Army fort, presumably this was Fort Gibson. Fort Gibson was one of many forts, now a garrison, along the former Louisiana Purchase that protected the western border of the United States. Fort Gibson was also used to protect the Indians from the east from hostile Osage and other Plains Indians. In this new land, Creek and Cherokee both had intertribal problems developing a system of government, especially when Chief Ross arrived from being force marched on the Trail of Tears and refused to acknowledge the Cherokee government of Indian Territory. Eventually, Colonel Matthew Arbuckle, the commander of the Seventh Infantry Regiment, which was assigned to Fort Gibson, helped to solve the problem

George walked up to the fort's entrance, and asked the two men guarding it, "Is this Fort Gibson?"

"Aye. State your business," replied the corporal to George's right.

"I've come to find out if anyone in my clan made it here when they were marched here last winter and I have business with others in my tribe,"

"How come you're just now getting here?"

"I got lost," George decided to answer with as little detail as he could get away with.

"I see. I'll escort you to the administration building and you can speak with the lieutenant in charge of the records. Follow me."

George followed the soldier to the administration building, went inside, and found their way to the records office. At the desk where a lieutenant was seated, the corporal said, "Lieutenant Perkins, this Indian needs to find out if anyone in his family made it here after their journey from back east,"

"Thank you, Mr. Johnson, you're free to return to your post,"

"Thank you, sir." Johnson saluted Perkins and left the office.

Perkins saluted back and then turned to George, "I'm Lieutenant Andrew Perkins, and you are?"

"I'm known as George Washington Massey,"

"That's an interesting name to have. So how did you manage to avoid the trek to Indian Territory?"

"I actually was on the forced march, but I tripped, causing me to fall and hit my head while we were in Kentucky. When I woke up, everyone who were still alive was gone.

I stumbled upon a white family that took me in, and I waited until late spring to come here to find out what happened to everyone I knew,"

"All right, that makes sense. Tell me the last name of your clan and I'll search the records,"

"Our Christian name is Massey. If you can't find Massey, they might be under our original Cherokee clan name, Etowah,"

Lieutenant Perkins went over to a large bookshelf that had a stack of books on each shelf. George could see that each shelf was labeled alphabetically. Perkins fumbled through the books until he found the records that started with both "E" and "M" and carried them over to his desk. Opening the "M" book first, Perkins looked for the name of Massey, but couldn't locate it. "I'm sorry, Mr. Massey, but there are no Massey's listed here,"

"I can't say I'm surprised, but it does hurt my heart a great deal to hear that none of them made it here. What about Etowah?"

Perkins opened the "E" record book and thumbed through it until he came near where Etowah might be. Again, he didn't find the name. "I'm sorry, it's not here either,"

"There must be someone left from my clan other than myself. Is there anywhere else I can go to find out?"

"I'm sorry, but there isn't, at least not in Indian Territory. The Cherokee government of Chief Ross has the same records we do, so that would be a dead end,"

George really wanted to sit down and cry for his people, but now really wasn't the time. Doing his best to remain calm, he decided to ask about someone else, "All right, is there a record for the Ahnikawi clan?"

"Hold on, let me put these two back and I'll get the book that holds the A's,"

After putting the other two record books back, Lieutenant Perkins returned with the "A" book. Placing it on the desk, he thumbed through it and found the Ahnikawi after asking George how to spell it. "Good news, that name is in here. Who are you looking for?"

"Does your records also have the individual surnames for the clan? It's because Ahnikawi are one of the larger clans of the Cherokee, while mine was one of the smallest,"

"Of course,"

"Good. Do you have a record for a woman named Adsila White Deer?"

Perkins scanned the pages and found the name George wanted to find. "Yes, here it is, Adsila White Deer. She lives near the town of Tahlequah,"

"Does the record happen to say where she lives?"

"Yes, let me write it down for you." Perkins wrote down the details, handed it to George, and asked, "Is there anything else I can help you with?"

"Do you know how far Tahlequah is from here?"

"I'd say about twenty miles,"

I wonder if I can rent a horse? Maybe someday there'll be some other means of travel that doesn't require a horse or walking and can get you there in an hour or two instead of days. George thought, since it would take him another day to get to Tahlequah if he walked that distance and he was getting impatient with being told to go here and there. "Do you know if the livery stable in town rents horses or if there even is one?"

"There is and I think they do, but I couldn't tell you how much they charge,"

"That's all right. What about hotels in town? Are there any?"

"Yes, there are hotels in Muskogee, and like all towns, there's the respectable establishments and the not-so-respectable,"

"Lieutenant, you've been a great help, thank you."

"You're welcome." Both men shook hands and George left the building, headed for a hotel so he could sleep on a bed, and get some restful sleep before heading to Tahlequah.

Chapter 9

George asked around the town of Muskogee about a hotel to stay in, one that was cheap, but respectable. The town being a Creek town, they viewed him as one of them, so they were very helpful and directed him to the only hotel he would be able to afford, since the other one was the saloon's rooms. George had no desire to sleep in such a noisy establishment, where there were saloon girls who would try to take what little money he had on him.

Walking inside the hotel, he was greeted by an elderly white man, with what sounded like a French accent, "Welcome. How can I help you?"

"I'd like a room for the night,"

"Good, we have a room available. It'll be five dollars,"

George thought five dollars was kind of expensive, since he had only fifteen dollars on him, but he wanted a good night's rest, so he paid the man. Then he asked, "Why are you running a hotel in Indian Territory? I can't imagine you'd have many visitors here,"

"I've been around here since my fur trading days, nearly thirty years now. We have many people from many different nations beyond the Atlantic traveling through these parts, more than anyone realizes. We have a lot of economic business from steamboats bringing goods here, some from the bigger ships in the Gulf of Mexico, so I get a lot of overnight travelers staying here. Anyway, here's your room key and I hope you sleep well."

"Thank you and good day." George went to his room, changed into night clothes, and even though it was two hours before sunset, he climbed into bed and fell asleep.

The next day, George woke up three hours after sunrise, realizing he was much more exhausted than he thought he was, but he did finally feel rested. Once he packed his things back up, he went downstairs, asked about breakfast, and the elderly man directed him to the hotel's small restaurant. George ordered breakfast, ate it quickly when it came, and then left the hotel so he could rent a horse from the livery.

At the livery, a Creek man, about George's age, was shoeing a horse, so George approached him, and asked, "Can I rent a horse from you?"

"You can. Where do you plan on going with the horse and for how long?"

"Right now, I plan on going to Tahlequah, probably for a day or two. How much will it cost me?"

"You know you won't get to Tahlequah until close to suppertime tonight, right?"

"I know,"

"I just wanted you to be aware of how long it'll take. I'll charge you three dollars for renting the horse, but I'll supply the tack and the saddle for free, as long as you return everything by Friday. Do we have a deal?"

"We have a deal."

"Good. I'll get the horse and I'll saddle him for you."

A few minutes later, the man brought out a saddled spotted chestnut colored Appaloosa. "All right, that'll be three dollars. Chestnut, which is what I call this horse, is calm and easy to work with. I expect to see you and him by the end of the week. Got it?"

"Got it. Thanks again." George mounted the horse and rode towards Tahlequah.

George heard through the grapevine that Tahlequah was now designated as the capital of ancestors of both the Cherokee Nation and United Keetoowah Band of Cherokee Indians. From what he remembered, the name of the town in Indian Territory was similar to the Cherokee town in Tennessee, called Talikwa. The name means, "The open place where the grass grows."

With the occasional break to rest the horse, letting him drink some water, and for both to have lunch, George arrived in Tahlequah just as the sun was setting. Chestnut was put up for the night in the town's livery and George found another respectable hotel. The hotel was three dollars cheaper than the hotel in Muskogee.

The next day, George decided to walk to Adsila White Deer's house because she lived less than a mile from the town center. He hadn't seen her in almost seven years, since they were nearly fourteen years old. Although he wanted to see her, George was also apprehensive and worried about how she might react to seeing her betrothed for the first time in so many years. He also wondered if she had ever become a Christian. He recalled that she was an attractive girl to look at and had an agreeable personality, so he hoped nothing had changed in these seven years.

George came to a house that was built in the log cabin design. In front, a garden was growing and there was a flowerbed underneath the end of the porch on the right side. Before he made it halfway across the path to the door, a woman came outside, but she apparently didn't see him. George thought she looked like an twenty-one year old version of Adsila, so he came closer, cleared his throat so she could hear him, and asked her in their native language, "Um, I'm looking for Adsila White Deer, you wouldn't happen to be her, would you?"

She looked at him and he looked vaguely familiar to her, but she couldn't place where they might have met before. "Yes, I'm Adsila, who are you?"

Taking a deep breath, George replied, "I'm George Massey,"

She went from having a curious look to looking like she'd just seen a ghost. Adsila sunk to the steps on the porch, and said, "I.... we.... my family thought we'd never see you again and assumed you were dead,"

"I'm not,"

"We just assumed you were, since we heard so many died on what our people are now calling the Trail of Tears,"

"I know and I grieve for them. However, some of my clan were supposed to have traveled here long before the forced march. Do you know what happened to them? There's no record of any of them at Fort Gibson,"

"I don't know. They could've been absorbed into the larger clans, because that's happened a lot since we arrived. There's also been some tension between the old and new settlers, especially between Chief Ross and Stand Watie's people, so much so that there's even talk of a split in the nation. I know I probably shouldn't ask, but why are you here?"

"Other than to find out what happened to my relatives, I came to honor the commitment our families made for us when we were young,"

"Oh, dear,"

"What's wrong?"

"You're no longer bound to the promise as my betrothed. You see, once I reached the appropriate age, I released you from that contract our parents made,"

"Oh." George felt disappointed and angry at the same time, since he felt stupid for assuming she'd wait for him. "You met another then?"

"I'm sorry, George, I really am. Had I known you were bound to come, I would've waited. But, years passed. I fell in love with someone and we finally married less than two years ago. I'm actually expecting our first child,"

"I see,"

"Please don't be angry with me, I did what I thought was right considering the circumstances. I really hope you understand,"

"I'm not angry at you, but I am disappointed and hurt. I should've probably thought this through more, since you're right, our peoples' circumstances forced a change in plans. I'm sorry I couldn't be here for you. I'm glad you found someone that makes you happy. Is your spouse worthy of you and does he treat you well?"

"Oh, yes, George. He treats me very well and has a good relationship with my family. If you would stay, I'll introduce him to you and we can have dinner together,"

George didn't even have to think about his answer, "Thank you, but I'll have to decline. It was nice seeing you Adsila and I pray that God continues to bless you and your family. Goodbye."

George turned and headed back towards town, leaving Adsila sad that she had to tell him the news and perplexed by his somewhat stand-offish demeanor, since she remembered George as someone who was always friendly and outgoing. When she could no longer see him, Adsila went inside to talk to her mother. "Ma, you'll never guess who I just saw,"

"You're right, I'll never guess. Who was it?"

"George Massey,"

"Really? I thought he was dead,"

"He's definitely alive and he wanted to know if any of his clan had managed to make it here. I had to tell him I didn't know. He also came to fulfill his duty of marrying me, since you and his folks made the betrothal when we were young,"

"Is he still here?"

"No,"

"What did you tell him? Did you tell him you were married?"

"Yes, I told him what he needed to know,"

"What happened after that? Do you know where he went?"

"I don't know, he just left, and he didn't tell me where he was going. All I know was that he was on the Trail of Tears, but he didn't tell me anything about what happened between then and now,"

"He mysteriously appears and then disappears again, that's very odd. Are you going to tell your husband?"

"No. I don't want him to feel threatened by George's visit or the fact that he's still alive, since he thinks George is dead. I'd appreciate it if you didn't tell him, Ma."

"I won't, I promise."

George went to the hotel to collect his things, and then went to the livery, had Chestnut saddled, and they rode off towards Muskogee. He did his best to not think of the hurt his heart felt and the pain from not knowing what happened to his clan affect him, otherwise, he thought he'd spend weeks in bed being depressed and he didn't want to do that. A few hours later, he returned Chestnut to the livery he rented the horse from and decided to sleep under the stars before he set off towards Fort Smith in the morning.

Nearly five days after leaving O'Hara's raft to go to Indian Territory, George returned to Fort Smith in the early evening. He figured he had at least a day or two before O'Hara was set to return back east. When he approached where the raft was tied up, George could see that O'Hara had sold all of his wares, and the only thing left on the raft were supplies. George didn't feel like searching for O'Hara in town, so he unbundled his bedding, laid it out, and then went to sleep as soon as he laid down.

O'Hara returned to his raft the next morning. He saw the sleeping George immediately, but decided not disturb him. The Irishman had sold everything he needed to sell a day earlier, so he was glad George returned when he did, because O'Hara was all set to return home. He hoped the young man found what he was looking for, but since George was here, the older man figured it probably hadn't worked out like the youngster wanted. He would let George tell him what happened when the young Cherokee was ready. In the meantime, O'Hara prepared the raft to leave so they could head home. An hour after the raft left the pier, George woke up, mostly from water splashing on him, and he told O'Hara a few days later what happened.

Chapter 10

Nearly three months after George left Paducah, he returned. The thought never crossed his mind to actually stay in Indian Territory after finding out the woman he was betrothed to was already married and thought he was dead. Then there was the fact that no one knew what happened to his clan. Were any living or were they all dead? George wasn't sure if that question would ever be answered. He didn't know when it happened, but he now thought of the McGregor's as family and also started thinking of Ellie as a woman he could get to know and marry someday. He hoped she felt the same way. As the raft neared Paducah, George was apprehensive because he wasn't sure what the McGregor's reaction to his return would be, but he would find out for better or worse.

O'Hara tied up the raft at one of the piers so George could get off, but the Irishman would continue eastward. "Good luck, George, I hope and pray that this time you find what you're looking for,"

"Thank you. I enjoyed your stories about Ireland and its tales and I pray that your trip home is safe and uneventful. Goodbye, Mr.

O'Hara." They shook hands and both went on their separate ways.

With great trepidation, George walked to the McGregor's, trying to not let his imagination get the best of him as he thought about various ways how it would end. His thoughts went from thinking they'd run him off their property while shooting at him, they might just ignore him, Duncan would haul him off to the sheriff and the town would hang him, to thinking they'd be happy to see him, but no longer wanted anything to do with him. George prayed for guidance and the wisdom to do the right thing.

He found the family working outside like they normally did and the first person to see him was Jacob, who excitedly shouted, "Hey! Look! George is back!"

The four McGregor's rushed over to him, took turns hugging him, and Duncan said, "Welcome back, George, we're all so glad to see you. We got your letter two weeks ago. I'm guessing it didn't turn out the way you hoped?"

George felt relieved that none of the scenarios in his imagination turned out to be true. He replied, "No, it didn't," and before he said another word, he began crying. George slowly and tearfully unburdened himself to the McGregor's about everything that happened on his trip. Once he let go of his troubles, George felt better.

"We're truly sorry for your loss, George. I think my husband and I agree that you're welcome to stay here as long as you need to. Right, Duncan?" Moira replied while hugging the grieving young man.

"Most definitely. Take all the time you need and if there's anything you need, we're here for you. If you need a fatherly figure to talk to, I can fulfill that role, if that's what you want,"

"Thanks everyone, you've been most kind to me and thank you for being so supportive, I appreciate it. All right, now that I'm back, do you need help with anything?"

"Listen, George, you should probably take some time to rest, and when you feel better, you're free to help us out wherever we need it. All right?"

"I guess I'll do that. Can I use the bed you let me use when I was here last?"

"Of course, it's ready for you." replied Moira.

"All right, thank you."

Most of the McGregor's started drifting off to go back to their chores, but Duncan stayed by George's side while he went to the house. "So, since you're no longer betrothed, have you given any thought to how my daughter feels about you?"

"Yes, I have, but I'm not really ready to court her right now. I'm glad she still feels the way she does about me,"

"I understand. When you need advice, her mother and I will give you that advice. Even though you left, I don't think Ellie ever gave up the idea that you might return, because she wrote you letters almost every other day. Unfortunately, she couldn't send them because we really weren't sure where to send the letters. When you're ready, I'm sure she'll let you read them. However, if you break my daughter's heart or treat her in any disrespectful way, you will no longer be welcome here. Understood?"

"Yes, sir."

Duncan slapped George on the back, and replied, "Good, we have an understanding. All right, I've got to get back to work, and we'll see you later."

Moira and Ellie watched the two while weeding the garden. Ellie asked, "Do you think George still likes me?"

"I think he might, you two got along really well before he left for Indian Territory. However, he was just rejected by his betrothed, so it might be a while before he comes around, so give him time, daughter,"

"I will. What do you think Pa's saying to him?"

"Knowing your father the way I do, I think he's telling George about how you feel, how your father feels about the situation, and what'll happen if George disrespects you. Remember, we have your well-being in mind when it comes to potential suitors, daughter, so don't be angry when we try to protect your honor from some of them."

"I understand, Ma." The two continued weeding the garden.

Two weeks later, George felt better about his situation and began to feel up to talking to Ellie about a possible courtship between the two. He found her milking the cow, so he asked, "Do you have time to talk?"

"Yeah, I'm almost finished. Do you want to help me take the buckets into the house?"

"All right."

She finished milking a few minutes later, George picked up two buckets, while Ellie carried one. On their way to the house, she asked, "So, what did want to talk about?"

Although George wanted to talk to her, some doubts crept into his thoughts about courting her, but having prayed for wisdom in this matter, George quickly dismissed the doubts. "Well, I was wondering if you were still interested in being courted,"

Ellie stopped in her tracks, not quite believing what she heard. *George finally wants to court me? I've been praying for this for so long, thank you, Lord Jesus! Now what do I do? Maybe I ought to ask Ma for more advice? Or maybe I ought to ask Laura, Thomas' wife, for advice. So many questions I have….*

"Um, Ellie, are you all right?"

"Huh? What?"

"Are you all right?"

Blushing, Ellie realized she'd been lost in thought. "I'm sorry, George, my thoughts ran away with me. Of course I want you to court me. Ma and Pa will want to hear about it, so let's go tell them!"

Ellie grabbed his hand and started to pull him towards where Duncan and Moira were, but George stopped her. "What about the milk? We can't just leave it out here, Ellie,"

"Oh! Right! Let's put it in the house, then we'll go tell my parents."

George stifled a laugh as they went into the house and put the buckets of milk on the table. *Ellie's definitely someone I want to be around. She's funny, a little scatter-brained, but in a good way, a good Christian girl, and loves life. I hope and pray we have a great life together. Now off to see her Ma and Pa.*

The two young people found Duncan and Moira, and both older adults had the vague idea they knew what this was about. Taking a deep breath, George said, "I'd like to ask for your permission to court your daughter,"

"What do you think, Moira? Should we approve?" Duncan had a hint of mischief in his eyes and tried not to crack a smile.

"Oh, I don't know. They really don't look like they like each other all that much. Are you two sure you want to court?" Moira winked at her husband because it was obvious the two young adults liked each other, they were holding hands and looked like a couple.

Ellie wasn't sure what to think. *Are they really against us? I'll do my best to convince them we want to be together.* "But, Ma and Pa, we do like each other and I want to spend the rest of my life with him. Don't you approve?"

Duncan and Moira burst out laughing, and Duncan said, "My dearest daughter, of course we approve, we were just joking with you. However, we do want to lay some ground rules so neither of you will get too carried away,"

"All right. What do you want us to do?" asked George.

"Let's go to the house so we can sit at the table and discuss what we want from you two. Let's go." Duncan replied.

In the house, the four sat down to discuss the parameters of George's and Ellie's courtship. Even though Ellie could do what she wanted now that she was seventeen, her parents always told her that she still lived under their roof, so she needed to follow their rules. She had no problem with her parents' decisions. Besides, her parents followed the advice of their parents as had her grandparents from their parents, and her brothers had done the same, so she thought if generations before her could follow the same courtship rules and be successfully married, so could she and George.

"All right, before we begin, I want the two of you to know that we don't ask any of this from you to be mean, but out of love, since we don't want you to make life altering mistakes many have over the years and centuries before they were married. Both of you understand, correct?" asked Duncan.

"Yes, sir," both replied.

"Good. First off, No more hand holding, which also includes hugging or kissing,"

George and Ellie let go of each other's hands and looked embarrassed.

"Next, whenever you two want to go somewhere, like a picnic or a town social, you need to have a chaperone. You can pick from anyone you know, including Moira and I, Jacob, Thomas and Laura, as long as the person or couple chaperoning you is responsible and won't leave you two alone. Now, do you two understand what we want from you?"

"Yes, sir," both replied.

"Great. I have one other thing to ask from you. I want the two of you to court for one year. When the year is through and we find that you're still together, George has permission to ask Ellie for her hand in marriage. Once you're engaged, we ask that you wait six months to marry. Are we agreed?"

Ellie and George looked at each other, and George asked her, "What do you think?"

"I don't have a problem with the rules. Do you?"

"No, I just wanted to make sure we were together on our promise. All right, we agree."

"I'm glad to hear that. George, I was also thinking of something else that would make sure you two stay pure. I think you should stay with Thomas and Laura, if they agree to the idea. You and I will ask them on Sunday after church. Are you agreeable with the idea?"

"If that's what you require from me, then I'll agree to it,"

"Good. We should pray for God's guidance on this issue as well. Dear Heavenly Father, we come to you this day to ask for you to guide George and Ellie as they get to know each other while courting. Please give them the wisdom to do what's right and if they are to marry, please help them to have a long, healthy marriage. Thank you for everything you do, amen. I have an idea. The next town social is on Independence Day, two weeks from now. The two of you will be able to spend the whole day together and we'll all have fun celebrating America's independence from England. Well, we've got to get back to our chores and we're burning daylight."

When Sunday came, Thomas and Laura agreed to let George live with them because they understood why it was necessary and George would also help Thomas in his store. George and Ellie were now almost limited to seeing each other on Sundays and special occasions, like holidays, but they were determined to make the courtship work.

Chapter 11

George was startled awake when he heard a cannon go off followed by the sounds of muskets. Thomas knocked on his bedroom door and said, "Hey, George, today's Independence Day. Come on sleepy head, get up. The rest of the family will be here shortly. You don't want to miss everything, do you?"

Yawning, George replied, "I'm getting up, I'll be out shortly."

While George dressed, he'd never experienced the Independence Day celebrations that those in the twenty-six states experienced, because the Cherokees ignored the event, having sided with the British during the War for Independence, with the consequences of that action being the eventual banishment to Indian Territory. This was in spite of the fact that the Cherokees decided to side with the Americans in the War of 1812, even though Chief Tecumseh and his confederacy of various tribal nations joined the British. George had heard about the political speeches, the parades, and the fireworks, but he'd never seen the spectacle. He was curious how the town celebrated the day of

America's independence and if they really did spend all day listening to speeches, which was something he wasn't too keen on doing.

Once dressed, he went to the dining room for breakfast, where Thomas and Laura were waiting. When he sat down, he asked, "Why were they shooting off a cannon and why were muskets being fired? Did someone attack?"

Thomas and Laura were surprised by the question and baffled by it. Thomas stopped eating to ask, "Did no one in your village shoot off a cannon at dawn to announce the arrival of Independence Day?"

"No. We didn't celebrate the event,"

"How come?" asked Laura.

"My people sided with the British during your war for independence. Even though it took sixty plus years, your government, still seeing us as enemies, even though we sided with your country in the War of 1812, paid us back by banishing my people to Indian Territory,"

"Oh."

"You know, that was President Jackson, along with his cronies who did that, not everyone in our country supported his actions. I didn't even vote for the man," replied Thomas.

"Still, it happened. However, I don't blame you or your family, as all of you have been kind to me and treated me like one of your own. I'll join your family while you celebrate, but I won't celebrate a country that would do what it did to my people."

"I guess I understand how you feel and I really don't want to start an argument. All right, let's finish our breakfast, the rest of the family should be here shortly."

Just as George finished breakfast, the rest of the McGregor's arrived and came into the house. Even though he was not really in the mood for celebrating, George made sure he didn't appear grumpy around Ellie. Wherever she went, George thought his betrothed lit up a room, her sunny attitude usually melted his heart, and before too long, he was in a better mood.

"The parade is about to start, let's go outside and watch." said Duncan.

The townspeople were gathered up and down the street where the parade took place. The air temperature was already in the upper seventies, the humidity was rising, and the sky clear of clouds. George could see a large platform near the courthouse that was built two days earlier, which would be where McCracken County officials and some state representatives would speak, since Paducah had no mayor as yet. Standing next to Ellie, George watched the parade.

First came the younger boys dressed in Revolutionary War outfits with their drums and other musical instruments playing patriotic songs. They were followed by a dozen very old men, some wearing the military uniform of the war. Ellie, being helpful, whispered to him, "They're some of the few remaining soldiers left from the War for Independence, all of them are nearing their nineties. I think we have a couple of soldiers living here who were in the War of 1812 too, but I don't know for sure."

Next came the men from this part of the state who were in the Kentucky militia. Following them, another band. After the band, state and local officials were next. The local officials were walking and the state officials were in carriages and waved to the crowd. Suddenly, everyone in the crowd became excited, and Ellie said to George, while pointing at the last carriage in the parade, "Pa said that's Henry Clay, our senator to the United States Congress. According to Pa, Clay's running for President of the United States for the second time, even though it's still a whole year away. I bet he's here to give a speech too."

Even George had heard about Henry Clay, he was a man that seemed to crave power. From being Speaker of Kentucky's House of Representatives to United States House of Representatives Speaker to being United States Secretary of State to creating the Whig Party. Clay created the Whig Party after being defeated as a National Republican in the election of 1832 when Jackson and the Democrats won. He helped settle a dispute about free and slave states called the Missouri Compromise of 1820. Clay also helped to defuse the nullification crisis between the federal government and South Carolina, which could've led to a war if South Carolina had followed through on seceding from the Union. Clay, along with John C. Calhoun, created an economic plan called the American System to compete with the British through tariffs. Eventually, Clay's ideas were opposed by President Jackson when Clay wanted the government to use the tariffs to improve infrastructure, like roads. Jackson opposed all of it because he thought it was unconstitutional, even though he sometimes ignored the Constitution himself. George wasn't sure he cared, since he wasn't allowed to vote and wasn't considered a citizen.

A few minutes later, the officials were sitting on stage, while all the men and a handful of women gathered to listen. The rest of the women were preparing food for their family picnic. The United States representative for the First Congressional District of Kentucky, Linn Boyd, was the first to come to the podium. After speaking for an hour about his role in Washington, his support of former President Andrew Jackson's policies, and his thanks to the citizens for electing him to the seat, he introduced Henry Clay as the next one to speak. Clay was known for his long-winded oratory, which could last longer than two hours if he was given enough leeway.

"Thank you for the introduction, Congressman Boyd. As you all know, we're celebrating the sixty-fourth anniversary of the War for Independence from England. We've gone through many challenges as a country in the last sixty-four years, but with God on our side, we've been able to overcome those challenges, including from some of our own countrymen. One of those challenges was from the previous executive in the White House who acted like a dictator. This is why I have again declared myself as a candidate for President of the United States in the election in 1840, so we can correct these mistakes Jackson and Van Buren have done to our country….."

Uninterested in hearing Senator Clay go on and on, George went to look for Ellie, who was helping her mother prepare their lunch. Both smiled at him when he walked up, he smiled back, and he asked Ellie, "Would you like to go for a walk?"

"What? Why?" Even though Ellie was helping her mother, she was doing her best to listen to the Senator's speech.

"Doesn't his speeches bore you?"

"If he goes on as long as he usually does, it will,"

"Moira, would you mind if Ellie and I go for a walk?"

"Not at all, George, but you need a chaperone,"

"Don't you still need help, Ma?"

"Not really, Ellie. Go off with your young man, I'll be fine,"

"Are you sure, Ma?"

"Yes, my daughter, I'm fine. Go have fun, but remember to be back here before Mr. Clay is through with his speechifying, probably in an hour or two."

"All right. We could ask Jacob to come along with us. I think he might be playing with some of his friends, so let's go find him,"

Thanks, Moira." said George.

Ellie and George found Jacob near the livery playing the game of Marbles with two other boys. Interrupting the boys, Ellie said to her brother, "Jacob, George and I are going for a walk and we need a chaperone. Want to go with us?"

"Do I get to tell on you if you break one of the rules Ma and Pa gave you?"

Ellie sighed, "Yes, you can, but if you make something up to get us into trouble, you better hide,"

Jacob crossed his heart, "I promise, I won't make something up. Fine, I'll go with you, besides, I'm losing." Then he stuck his tongue out at the other boys, who did the same.

The three headed off towards the woods, while Ellie and George talked. Ellie asked, "Do you know what you want to do for a living? Like own your own farm?"

"I'm not entirely sure what I want to do. I enjoy helping Thomas and Rachel with the store, so I might do that and open a store out west somewhere. I'm sure I don't want to farm. There's too much reliance on the weather cooperating, praying that a natural disaster doesn't happen, along with hoping that market prices stay stable to make a profit. Farming is just too backbreaking for too little money. I decided that I want to have enough money to where I'm not so easily pushed around by people more powerful than myself. Does that make sense?"

"Yes, it does. Pa constantly worries about hail, tornadoes, fire, grasshoppers, drought, and also watches the markets because he hopes a panic doesn't happen this year or next. Farming is too stressful, so if you want to be a storekeeper, I'll support you,"

"I'm glad to hear it. I'll have to save some money from what your brother pays me and maybe we'll have plenty of money to move west and open a store, although, I'm not sure where out west at the moment,"

"I think the Lord will provide the answer when it's time, all you have to do is continue working towards your goal."

"I think so too."

Ellie and George continued walking in silence for a while, with Jacob trailing behind them. Jacob made sure to keep his eyes on his sister and George to make sure they didn't do something they weren't supposed to be doing. After about an hour and a half of walking through the woods, then along the river, skipping stones across the water, dipping their toes into the cool water, and enjoying each other's company, George, Ellie, and Jacob came back to town just as Senator Clay was finishing his speech.

"And remember folks, the Whig Party will be holding its first ever convention in

December to nominate their candidate for President of these United States, so I expect I will be your nominee when we defeat Martin Van Buren in November of next year. Thank you for listening today, have fun with your Independence Day celebration, and may God Bless America. I'll now yield to the next speaker."

The assembled crowd cheered and clapped, some mostly because Clay was finally finished, while others truly enjoyed his speech. When the convention is held in December, Clay loses the Whig nomination to William Henry Harrison.

Ellie, George, and Jacob found Duncan emerging from the crowd as it dispersed twenty minutes later when the last speaker finished, and when he saw the three, he smiled. Then he said, "I'm glad that's over with. Clay's a gifted, but long-winded orator. There are times I wish we could vote for U.S. Senators, because I think I'd vote for someone other than Clay. Now for the most important activity of the day – lunch. Do you think your Ma has the meal ready yet?"

"I don't know, but I'm hungry enough to eat a horse!" replied Jacob.

Laughing, Duncan replied, "All right, let's go find your Ma and eat her delicious food. Come on."

The four found Moira had already set out the blanket they'd be sitting on, while the food looked prepared to eat. Duncan gave Moira a kiss, and she said, "I'm glad the speeches are over with, my food was starting to get cold. Before we dig in, let's pray over the food. Go ahead, Duncan."

"Lord, we thank your for the great weather you've given us as we eat this meal on a holiday where we celebrate our country's independence. Please give our leaders the wisdom to lead this country the way you'd like them to and they'll acknowledge you in everything. Thank you for my family and thank your for bringing George into our lives. In your name, amen. All right, let's eat."

After everyone in town ate their picnic lunches, they played games, raced horses, and even square danced until it was time for the fireworks. George watched the fireworks with awe, since he'd never seen such a display before, and he thought the various ways the fireworks went off was amazing. Overall, even though he was not too enthused about celebrating America's independence at the beginning of the day, he had an enjoyable day nonetheless.

Chapter 12

The year of their courtship went by quickly for Ellie and George. To them, it seemed like only a few weeks, instead of fifty-two. They spent most of their courtship going on picnics or attending town socials. George continued working for Thomas and Laura in the store, saving as much as he could, but still a ways off from being able to build a store of his own. He was thinking of going west eventually, since the Oregon and California Trails were slowly opening up to anyone who wanted to go west and he figured they'd need people who knew how to supply the settlers. However, that was sometime in the future, because his first commitment was to Ellie.

The day of their final day of courtship finally arrived. The entire family was set to have dinner together and George was nervous because he was planning something that Ellie probably wouldn't know was coming. Earlier in the day, he went to Duncan, and asked, "Duncan, I'd like to talk to you about my future with Ellie. I love her and I want to ask your permission to marry her,"

"You have my permission. However, how's your financial situation and what are your plans for the future?"

"Financially, I think I'm secure. I'm saving money for our marriage and also so I can build a general store in the future, probably out west,"

"If you plan on going west, I hope you know that starting from scratch is difficult, and love won't always get you through those hard times,"

"I do know that. I think Ellie and I are prepared for difficult times, but I guess one never knows until they have to go through it,"

"You're right, you won't know until it happens. George, I think you're probably as prepared as you can be to marry my daughter. Remember, the engagement should last six months before the marriage, mostly because it's customary. All right?"

"I understand. Thank you for giving your permission."

After the family dinner, George turned to Ellie, and said, "I have something to ask you." He got down on the floor, kneeled down on one knee, pulled out a small box, and opened it, which revealed a diamond ring. Thomas had helped George pick out a diamond ring through mail order after George had saved enough money. Ellie gasped and started crying, while George continued, "Elizabeth Jane McGregor, will you marry me?"

Nodding her head, she replied, "Oh, yes! Yes, I will!" Without thinking, she kissed George, then realized what she did, blushed, and said, "Oops,"

"Don't worry, Ellie, you have permission to kiss him now that you're engaged, but there are still things we would prefer you wait 'til marriage for," replied Duncan.

"Thank you, Pa. George and I have pledged to wait, so you don't need to worry about that. Ma, do you think we could go see Mrs. Bowen tomorrow to see if we can't use the church for the wedding and the reception?"

"That's a great idea. We can go to the dressmaker too so she can start working on your wedding dress,"

"I'm not sure that's a good idea, Ma,"

"Why not?"

"Because she sneers at me and George whenever we walk past her. Sometimes, when she's talking with other women whenever George and I are in town together, they do a lot of whispering back and forth, and then some of the other women have looks in their eyes like they hate the two of us,"

"Well, it wouldn't hurt to ask her, she'll probably say no and that would be that. I'd let you use mine, but it's rather frail, and you deserve a new dress. If all else fails, we can order fabric through Thomas' store and I'll make your dress myself,"

"Ma, I don't want to put any undue burden on you,"

"My dear daughter, don't worry about it. I would enjoy creating your wedding dress if the dressmaker refuses,"

"Thanks, Ma." Ellie hugged Moira.

"You're very welcome, Ellie."

The next day, Ellie and Moira went to the pastor's house to talk to his wife, Jennifer. She welcomed them into the house and asked, "So, what's the purpose of this visit?"

"Well, I'm now engaged, so Ma and I were wondering if you and Pastor Bowen would allow us to get married in the church and have the reception there,"

"Engaged? To who?"

"You know who, Mrs. Bowen, George Massey,"

"Oh, I see," Jennifer Bowen went from smiling to looking ashen.

"That's not the reaction we were expecting, Jennifer," admonished Moira.

"I'm sorry. Letting you and George use the church won't be possible, for a number of reasons,"

"I'm sure I can guess why you won't let us and those reasons aren't very good excuses for people who claim they're Christians and lead this church," Ellie angrily replied.

"Would you care to explain, Jennifer?" Moira asked, before Mrs. Bowen had the chance to say something sarcastic to Ellie.

"I suggest you ask your husband and your future son-in-law to take that up with my husband. I have no more to say on this matter. Is there anything else you'd like to talk about?"

Looking at Ellie, Moira could tell her daughter was simmering with anger. It was a rare event when she let her anger get the best of her, but woe to those who made her angry. Hoping to leave the Bowen house before Ellie decided to say what she really thought and would eventually regret, Moira replied, "No, there's nothing else we need to talk about. We'll show ourselves out. Goodbye." Moira grabbed Ellie by the arm and left the house.

Outside, Moira said to her daughter, "You need to calm down, because blowing your top won't do either of us any good.

Take a minute to pray and then we'll go visit the dressmaker,"

"But what about not being able to use the church?"

"Duncan and George will talk with Pastor Bowen and I'm sure everything will get straightened out. In the meantime, we'll plan your wedding,"

"If you say so, Ma." Ellie then closed her eyes, took some deep breaths, and looked like she was praying. When she was finished, she said, "All right, let's go visit the dressmaker and see what she has to say."

The two women walked down the street to where the dressmakers shop was. The dressmaker, Greta Johansson, was a widow, her husband had died ten years earlier from some kind of an accident that the McGregor's knew nothing about. After her husband's death, Mrs. Johansson went into business for herself making all sorts of dresses for the womenfolk of town who were too busy with their own children and/or farm work to do it themselves. She had a reputation as a gossip.

The two women entered the shop, and Johansson asked, "Good morning. How can I help you?"

"Good morning. I'm going to be married in a few months and I want to have a wedding dress made. Will you be able to do that?" Ellie asked.

"Are you the girl who's seeing that Indian?"

"If you mean George Massey, then yes,"

"Sorry, I can't help you,"

"Why?"

"I don't believe in mixed marriages, especially with those savage Indians. I'm surprised you still have your scalp…."

"Excuse me?" Ellie interrupted, feeling the anger rise in her once again.

"Indians take scalps and do all sorts of savage things,"

"Lady, you're wrong. The French fur trappers were the scalp takers and the Indians out west who interacted with them started following their lead. My George would never do such a thing,"

"What difference does it make? The only good Indian is a dead Indian,"

Even though Moira was also mad, she said, "Uh, we'll take our business elsewhere. Ellie, let's go to the store to order the supplies,"

Ellie's face was red with anger, almost as red as her hair, tears streamed down her cheeks, and her mother could see the wheels turning in her mind about how she could respond. So, before Ellie could reply to the dressmaker in anger and again regret it later,

Moira pulled her out of the store. They heard Mrs. Johansson say "Good riddance" before the door closed.

Walking towards Thomas' and Rachel's store, Ellie said, "Ma, I swear, if she said one more hateful thing, I was going to rip her hair out,"

"Please calm down. I'm angry too, but beating her up won't change her attitude,"

"Probably not, but it would make me feel better,"

"Maybe for a short while, then you'd regret it and wish you hadn't. Don't let it bother you, because there are people like her all over the place, and if you let each of them make you mad, they've won. Understand?"

"Yes, Ma, but I don't have to like it,"

"Very true, but you can pray that God helps you deal with those situations, and He'll help you. Once you feel He's helping, you just let go and let Him deal with it. All right?"

"Fine."

George, Thomas, and Rachel were busy in the store when Ellie and Moira entered. George could see immediately that something was wrong with Ellie - her face was nearly as red as her hair and she was teary-eyed. They hugged and he asked, "What's wrong?"

"Everything,"

"What do you mean?"

"She means that Jennifer Bowen says that her husband won't let you use the church for your wedding. Then when we went to the dressmaker, she refused to make a dress, and even said some hateful things as part of her refusal," replied Moira.

"Is there anything I can do to change their minds?"

"Well, you and Pa could talk to Pastor Bowen about why he refuses to marry us, but if you want to talk to Mrs. Johansson, I think you'd be wasting your time," replied Ellie.

"All right, I'll go get Duncan and we'll talk to the pastor. Thomas, do you mind if I leave?"

"No, I don't mind. Take care of my sister and your problems first, that's what's important."

"Thanks. I'm going to go get your Pa. Ellie, are you going to stay here?"

"Yes, I'll stay here. Ma and I are going to look through the catalogs for fabric we can use to make a wedding dress. Love you."

"Love you too." They kissed and George left the store.

George found Duncan and Jacob going through the fields looking for weeds. "Duncan, we have a problem,"

"What's wrong?"

"Ellie and Moira went to ask Mrs. Bowen about using the church and she said no. She also said that you and I ought to talk to her husband to find out the specific reasons. Do you have time?"

"They refused? Yeah, we need to talk to Bowen. Jacob, do you think you can handle this particular chore without me?"

"Sure, Pa."

"All right, George, let's go."

George and Duncan stepped into the church half an hour later and headed directly for Pastor Bowen's office. His door was open, so Duncan cleared his throat, and said, "Pastor, we need to speak with you,"

Bowen wasn't surprised by the visit, Jennifer came by an hour earlier to tell him she was visited by Ellie and Moira, so he was expecting the men of the family to show up to give him a piece of their minds. "Come in and please sit down." When they sat, he began speaking, "I know why you're here and no amount of pleading will change my mind,"

"Why not?" George asked.

"To be perfectly honest with you, there's too many in our church who have a problem with you and Ellie being a couple. Most of them didn't have a problem with you attending our church, but your betrothal was a little too far for them. There have been threats from the more powerful church members to fire me or talk of a split in our church if I were to let you use this building for your marriage ceremony. While I don't have a problem with joining you and Ellie in matrimony, I can't do it here,"

"You're a coward,"

"George!" Duncan exclaimed, not expecting his future son-in-law to say that.

Bowen shrugged and simply said, "If you were in my position, you would be too. Sorry,"

Getting up from his chair so he could leave, George replied, "You're sorry? Why don't I believe you? Some Christian leader you are, letting your congregation lead you instead of you leading it. In spite of these complications, Ellie and I are going to marry. Goodbye." George walked out of the office.

Duncan got up to leave too and was almost out of the office when Bowen said, "I really am sorry, Duncan, but that's just how things are. I hope you understand,"

"No, I don't understand. I hope you develop your backbone someday, otherwise, you'll have all sorts of church members

walk all over you for being so weak.
Goodbye,"

"Will we see you on Sunday?"

"We'll see." Duncan walked out of the
church.

Outside, George was waiting. He looked
like he could blow up, but was managing to
keep his cool. Duncan wondered what
would happen if George and Ellie ever got
mad at each other because of their tempers
and if it was just their lack of maturity that
caused them to go off the deep end so
quickly. He hoped he would never have to
find out.

While they walked towards the store,
George asked, "What are we going to do?
We need someone to marry Ellie and I,
because I'm not sure I trust Bowen right
now,"

"There are other preachers in town,
although not of the same denomination as
we are, but we could always find out how
they feel. Although, if we do that, our
dispute with our church will get around
town. I don't think we ought to be the ones
to instigate the inevitable gossip that's sure
to go around because of it,"

"Yeah, you're probably right. Maybe
Ellie and I ought to take some time to cool
off and then ask Pastor Bowen if he can
marry us. Maybe we can do it outdoors, near

the river, during the spring, even though that would extend the engagement by three months. What do you think?"

"Sounds like a plan. Talk to Ellie and then she and Moira can plan it out to their hearts delight,"

"What are you going to do about attending Bowen's church in the meantime?"

"Oh, we'll go, otherwise, the gossipers will come up with all sorts of juicy, outrageous gossip if we don't. We can't have that, you know. Besides, while I'm disappointed in Bowen and his lack of backbone, there are no other churches in our denomination that are within a day's distance from Paducah. If we go to any other church in Paducah, that'll set tongues wagging too, staying at Bowen's church is currently our only choice." Not knowing what else to say, Duncan said, "Well, let's go get Moira and Ellie and go home for supper."

Chapter 13

Over the next few months, Ellie and George prepared for their wedding. After receiving the fabric for Ellie's dress, Moira went to work creating the dress. She spent a lot of time on the dress because she wanted it to be better than her own wedding dress. Occasionally, Moira took Ellie's measurements to make sure the dress was fitted properly. Whenever Ellie tried it on, she exclaimed how beautiful it was and how nervous she was as the big day approached.

Ellie's birthday was coming up and George wanted to do something for her. Paducah was growing because of the river trade, so a theater house was built for the townsfolk to experience some culture. When it opened, Ellie once mentioned to George, "Someday, I'd like to go see one of those operas or Shakespearean plays that travel from town to town. I think it would be interesting to see one of those at least once."

George also overheard Ellie say to her mother while the dress was in the process of being made, "Ma, I'd really love to have a headpiece for this dress, too bad I can't afford one."

"We'll do the best we can, my daughter, maybe you'll end up with one when you least expect it,"

"I hope so."

George thought that a headpiece would be another good idea for a present, mainly to present to Ellie for a wedding gift. He went to Moira to ask about it, she happily described what her daughter wanted, and told him to order the headpiece through Thomas at the store. Even though it wouldn't arrive until a month or two after Ellie's birthday, he knew she would be happy with it no matter what.

George bought tickets to an opera that would be showing the day before Ellie's birthday. He prepared a picnic lunch with the help of Moira and Rachel and took her to their favorite spot. While they were eating, George said, "Ellie, I have a surprise for you,"

"What is it?"

George pulled out two tickets from his shirt pocket, "We have tickets to go see the opera tonight,"

Her eyes went wide with surprise, "Really?"

"Yes, I wanted to do something special for your birthday. I hope this is what you wanted."

"Oh, yes, very much so. Thank you, George. I look forward to going. You're so romantic!" She gave him a quick kiss.

That night they went to the opera, which was presented by an English troupe, Anne and Edward Seguin. They and others traveled across the United States and performed various operas for the American people. Even though opera was popular, George found it boring, but he loved Ellie and would do whatever she wanted and buy her whatever she needed. George knew she would love the headpiece once she received it and he decided he would give it to her before their wedding as a gift. Ellie was happy with her gift of the opera and loved George all the more for being so thoughtful, caring, and mindful of her likes and dislikes. She prayed that they would have a long, happy marriage, filled with children and laughter.

A little later, George was pondering where he and Ellie would go once they were married. He wanted to go west, but wasn't sure just how to do it, until he read an advertisement in the newspaper at the end of January before their marriage in March. The advertisement said that a wagon train would be organized in Independence, Missouri, and it would be set to leave in the middle of May, 1841. It continued on to say that the wagon train would be led by Thomas "Broken Hand" Fitzpatrick, a famous mountaineer who was also leading Jesuits to Montana, and he would lead the train to Fort Hall. Once at Fort Hall, the wagon train would continue on to either Oregon or California, depending on the travelers, with Fitzpatrick guiding the Oregon bound travelers. At the end of the advertisement, it asked anyone interested to show up in Independence before May and to be prepared for the long journey. After reading the advertisement, George saw another one about wagons being sold by the local blacksmith in Paducah, which was the solution to the problem of where to get a wagon.

First, George went to the blacksmith. The man was pounding some kind of metal piece on his anvil when George approached. Indicating to George to give him a minute, the blacksmith continued working until he placed the metal piece in a bucket, which crackled and steamed as it hit the water in the bucket. Wiping his brow, he asked, "Whatcha need?"

"Well, I need to buy a covered wagon, and I saw an advertisement in our paper that said you offer that service,"

"Aye, but I get it through mail order from the Studebaker Brothers in Ohio. It usually takes about a month after they receive the order for the parts to get here. Once that happens, it takes a few days to put it together. Still interested?"

"Of course and I'll help. Do I need to pay for it now?"

"No, you do that when the order arrives and we put it together. It'll cost you about one hundred dollars,"

"All right. Let's order it." George, not fazed by the price of the wagon, since he had more than enough money to cover the cost, gave the blacksmith his name and the blacksmith said he would send the order right away. George thanked the man and went on his way.

George told Ellie the plans. "Ellie, I think I know where we should go after we get married,"

"Where?"

"I saw an advertisement in the newspaper about a wagon train being organized to go to Oregon, while part of it plans on going to California. I think we ought to go to California. Anyone interested is supposed to show up in Independence, Missouri by May,"

"While I think that's a good idea, how do you propose to get there? We don't have a covered wagon, you know,"

"Actually, I just ordered a covered wagon from the blacksmith. It should take a month or so before the parts arrive, he and I will put it together, and it'll only cost a hundred dollars,"

"What about oxen and supplies?"

"We'll take care of the oxen when the wagon's completed. The supplies will have to wait until shortly before we leave,"

"So, do you think we'll leave for Independence right after we get married?"

"I think we ought to, since it's over four hundred miles from here and would take a little over a month overland if we go ten miles a day,

"My love, it sounds like you've thought of everything. I'll miss my family, but we're not exactly welcome by most of the people here, so maybe we'll be successful out west. Someday, maybe we could even get Ma and Pa to come to California when it's safe to travel for people their age,"

"We'll just have to see. I have to get to work, see you later." George kissed her and went back to town.

A week before the marriage, the disassembled wagon arrived at the blacksmith's shop. George paid for it and helped the blacksmith put the wagon together. When they finally assembled the wagon two days later, Duncan came to

George, and said, "You've completely assembled the wagon, right?"

"Yes, I'll have to go buy oxen too so I can bring the wagon to your property and store all of it here until after Ellie and I are married,"

"The oxen are what I want to talk to you about. Moira and I are going to buy you and Ellie a pair as a wedding gift,"

George was shocked, he wasn't expecting to hear what Duncan just said. The only reply he could think of was, "Really?"

"Yep, I think that's the least we could do for our daughter and her future husband as you two begin your future together. If there's anything else we can do for you, all you have to do is ask."

"Thank you, Duncan. Well, let's get to town and take care of business."

The two men went to the livery to take a look at the oxen Duncan bought for George. To George, the oxen looked strong and healthy and he hoped they survived the journey across the plains and mountains. George led the oxen to the wagon, hooked them up, and then led them to the store. At the store, George, Duncan, and Thomas loaded merchandise for George's future store that could be easily transported to California. Once they were through with that, George took the wagon to the McGregor farm until George and Ellie were ready to use the oxen and wagon after they were married.

Four days later, the young couple were ready to get married. In spite of not liking Pastor Bowen, they decided to let him marry them. Bowen had really been surprised by the request and wouldn't have done it if Ellie and George hadn't mentioned they'd be leaving Paducah. Now no one in town would hold it against him for marrying the two. The wedding would be outdoors in a meadow near the Ohio and the reception would be as well. Although Ellie sent out official invitations, only three families in Paducah sent in their replies that they would be attending. Duncan would give Ellie away, while Rachel would be her matron of honor, and Thomas would be George's best man.

The day before the wedding, Ellie was in for a surprise. Her parents sent her to the steamboat dock in Paducah, making her wonder why she was there. She didn't have to wait long to find out. As the passengers disembarked, she saw her brother, Caleb, departing the boat with a woman holding his hand. She had dark hair, tanned skin, and looked to be about two or three inches shorter than Caleb. Ellie ran over to them, hugged her brother, and said, "It's so good to see you, Caleb. I didn't know you were coming,"

"We wanted to surprise you and I guess we did a good job. Oh, you haven't met my wife, Sarah. Sarah, this is my only sister, Ellie,"

The two shook hands. "Howdy, Ellie, I'm glad to meet you. Caleb's told me so much about you and your family, I feel like I know ya'll already,"

"I'm pleased to meet you too. Caleb's letters told us about you and nearly everything that happens in Texas. By the way, where's your child?"

"Oh, we thought this would be a long trip for Lucas, being only a year old, so we left him with his grandparents back in Texas,"

"I understand, but Ma and Pa will be disappointed that they can't meet their first grandchild,"

"Yeah, I know, but they'll get to meet him later when he's a little older and can travel easier. Now, let's go meet your future husband." replied Caleb.

Once they were introduced, Caleb told George, "Did you know that the first President of Texas, Sam Houston, was married to a Cherokee? He was still married to his first wife, even though they were separated, and I'm pretty sure he's divorced from both by now. The Cherokee woman didn't accompany him to Texas though and I don't know what happened to her,"

"No, I didn't know that. My people tend to be open to mixed marriages. Chief Ross, the overall head of the Nation, was a product of one himself,"

"That is interesting. I wonder how many people in the future will claim Cherokees as their ancestors? I'm willing to guess there'll be a lot. Anyway, Sarah and I are somewhat fatigued from our trip, so we're going to rest a while before dinner."

Before George had to go home for the evening, he and Ellie finally got some alone time, he presented her with the gift he'd been waiting two months to give her – the headpiece for her wedding dress. He handed her a box, and said, "I hope you like this. It's for the wedding,"

Ellie gave him a questioning look as she took the box. She couldn't even begin to figure out what it was, until she opened it, and found the headpiece inside. She squealed like a little girl, pulled the headpiece out of the box, and tried it on. It fit her perfectly. The headpiece had a lace veil, with material that came from the back of the veil and descended nearly to the floor. There were also silk flowers and pearls lacing the edge of the headpiece at the top.

With tears in her eyes, she hugged George, and said, "This is amazing, thank you so much! I love you and I am so glad we're getting married tomorrow." Ellie gave George a big hug and kissed him.

"Ellie, I will do anything for you, I hope you know that. I love you with all my heart and you make me very happy. I love you too."

The next day was warm, sunny, and cloudless. Thirty guests were seated and the wedding party was in their places when the wedding march began. The march was played on the fiddle by Caleb, which was a surprise since the wedding originally had no music accompaniment for Ellie's march down the aisle. Duncan accompanied Ellie down the aisle and handed her off to George when the two finally stood in front of Pastor Bowen. George thought Ellie looked beautiful in her white wedding dress and Ellie thought George looked handsome in his black suit.

Pastor Bowen began speaking, "We're gathered here together on this happy and joyous occasion, to witness the joining of these two young people, George Massey and Elizabeth McGregor. Now, marriage is a solemn institution to be held in honor by all, it is the cornerstone of the family and of the community. It requires of those who undertake it a complete and unreserved giving of one's self. It is not to be entered into lightly, as marriage is a sincere and mutual commitment to love one another. This commitment symbolizes the intimate sharing of two lives and still enhances the individuality of each of you.

"Will you, George Massey, have Elizabeth McGregor to be your wife? Will you love her, comfort and keep her, forsake all others, and remain true to her as long as you both shall live?"

"I will,"

"Will you, Elizabeth McGregor, have George Massey to be your husband? Will you love him, comfort and keep him, forsake all others, obey him, and remain true to him as long as you both shall live?"

"I will,"

"Then repeat after me: I, George Massey, take thee Elizabeth McGregor, to be my wife, and before God and these witnesses, I promise to be a faithful and true husband,"

George repeated the words, then Pastor Bowen told Ellie to say the same words, and she repeated the words. Pastor Bowen continued, "George, will you put the ring on her finger, and then repeat after me: With this ring, I thee wed. In sickness and in health, in poverty or in wealth, 'til death do us part,"

George repeated the words to Ellie. Then Ellie was given the ring she was to slip onto George's finger, and then she repeated the words that Bowen told her to say. Once that was done, Bowen said, "In accordance with the laws of the Commonwealth of Kentucky and of God, I now pronounce you husband and wife. George, you can now kiss your bride."

The two kissed until they heard Pastor Bowen and Duncan clearing their throats. Ellie and George stopped and looked embarrassed because they'd gone a little too long with the kissing.

"Now it's time for the reception." replied Moira.

Everyone enjoyed the food and the music from the guests who had their own instruments, wished George and Ellie a happy marriage, and vowed they would pray for the two on their journey west. The next day, the new Mr. and Mrs. Massey would be leaving for Independence.

Chapter 14

Early the next morning, George and Duncan prepared the wagon and the oxen for the trip to Independence. The two men attached a barrel full of grain for the oxen on the side of the wagon, along with four barrels full of water for drinking, and packed enough food for the newlyweds that would last until they arrived in Independence. Moira, Rachel, and Sarah helped Ellie pack her belongings, but made sure not to pack so many things that it would bog down the wagon.

As they prepared to leave, Moira asked her daughter, "Please write to us when you get to Independence so we know you arrived safely, all right?"

"I'll do that, Ma. I'll even write down everything we see or experience while we're on the California Trail, and we'll send you those when we get to California,"

"We'll look forward to reading your letters."

"I think we ought to pray before your journey," stated Duncan.

"Good idea, my husband, would you lead the prayer?"

"All right. Heavenly Father, we thank you for the good times we've had with our family. We thank you for bringing George into our lives and thank you for letting him and Ellie find each other. We pray for a hedge of protection for them and for travel blessings as they traverse the great expanse to California. Give them the wisdom to do what's right. In all these things we do, we thank you for giving us the ability to do them. We thank you for sending your son to die on the cross for our sins. In your name, we pray, amen."

After everyone said their goodbyes, many hugs exchanged, and tears shed, George assisted Ellie onto the wagon, while George would be on foot and guiding the oxen. When the oxen began to pull the wagon, George and Ellie waved at the family and they waved back. The McGregor's continued watching until they could no longer see the wagon.

A few hours after they crossed the Mississippi River on a cheap ferry that amounted to little more than a raft guided by ropes, George said, "I'm sorry we didn't go on our honeymoon first, but time was of the essence."

"Don't worry about it, George, I understand. All that matters is that we love each other. Wherever you go, I'll go."

From the last three days of March and then into the first week of May, the newlyweds experienced one snowstorm, some heavy rain, some hail, heavy winds, and three days where it was hotter and more humid than normal. Even though George wanted to travel ten miles a day, some days they couldn't travel more than five miles, so he made up for that by having them travel from dawn to dusk for a week, with multiple breaks. Their oxen had no problem pulling the wagon over muddy trails and muddy roads. The wagon itself was sturdy and the canvas covering the wagon never once leaked. The couple spent many nights sleeping in the wagon because of the waterproofed canvas. Every day, besides doing their daily Bible devotions, they prayed for protection and traveling mercies. Ellie did what she told her mother she would do and recorded their experiences. Once they reached Independence, she would send it all in a letter to her parents.

During the wildly various weather conditions, Ellie was filled with uncertainty, and asked, "Do you think we're doing the right thing?"

"I think we are, but we won't really know until we get to California safe and sound. I don't think the weather should stop us, since we're both healthy and strong.

We'll succeed with God's help. Please don't worry, we'll make it."

When they finally arrived in Independence, the two newlyweds saw that the town was nearly as busy as Paducah. Freight wagons were everywhere, people walking or riding on horseback to and fro trying to get to one place or another, but the Massey's didn't see one hint of a wagon train. Not knowing what else to do, George guided the wagon to the livery, where he saw a black boy, about ten years old, cleaning out horse pens, so he asked him, "Hey there. Have you heard of a man named Thomas Fitzpatrick? He's supposed to be assembling a wagon train that's going west,"

"Sure have, Mister. He's got a whole mess of wagons with a few dozen people about a mile west of here near the Missouri River. You can't miss 'em,"

"Thanks. Where's the general store so I can buy some supplies?"

"Just down the street, Mister. It's easy to find,"

"Do you know where the post office is?" asked Ellie.

"Yes'm. It's behind the livery on the next street, where the stagecoaches stop to let people off,"

"Thank you, we appreciate your help. Here's something for your trouble." George tossed the boy a dime.

A smile spread across the boy's face, he inspected the dime, then said, "Thanks, Mister." Then the boy put the dime in his pocket and continued working.

"What do you want to do first, Ellie? Go to the post office or the general store? Or, do you think we ought to meet up with the others on the wagon train?

"The post office is just around the corner. I'll go there and you go to the general store. I'll catch up with you there. All right?"

"All right, we'll do that." George helped Ellie step off the wagon, she kissed him, and walked over to the next street over. Next, George guided the oxen to the general store.

Ellie found the Post Office easily enough, but saw that the American flag in front of the building was at half-staff. When she went inside and walked up to the clerk so she could send the letter, she first asked, "Why's the flag at half-staff? Did something horrible happen?"

The man rolled his eyes. "Where have you been? President Harrison died a little over three weeks ago from pneumonia. He took the oath of office in cold, wet weather, wasn't wearing an overcoat or a hat, and spoke for two hours before riding on horseback in the parade in that same weather. From there, he developed a nasty cold and then pneumonia. Now, John Tyler's our President,"

"I'm truly sorry to hear that. My husband and I have been traveling for the past month and haven't heard any news. It's truly a shame and may God rest his soul. Um, the reason that I'm here is because I need to send a letter to Paducah, Kentucky,"

"Fine, we'll send it out on the next stage. Is there anything else I can do for you?"

Ellie handed the clerk the letter. "No, thank you. Good day."

"Good day."

Ellie found George loading the food they'd need for the five to six month journey onto the wagon. She told him about President Harrison, then George said, "I heard. Some men in the store were discussing what happened. Now that Tyler's the President of the United States, one of the men thought he'd try to get Texas into the Union. Another man thought if that happened, Mexico would go to war with the United States, no matter how ineffectual the Mexican Army can be, and in spite of the fact that Spain controlled the land, while Mexico really never did. He even said an Indian tribe in the southwest, called the

Apache, could even defeat the Mexicans if they were properly equipped, because those Indians were supposed to be really savage warriors,"

"Did you say anything to the men?"

"No, they wouldn't want to hear from me, since they'd consider me a savage Indian, and I'd rather stay out of it,"

"I'm glad you want to stay out of it, because we don't want any trouble, and I don't want anyone to hurt you. Have you finished stocking the wagon?"

"Yes. Besides the food, I also bought two more wagon wheels besides the one we already have, an extra axle, more ammunition for my gun, and spare repair tools in case we lose any on our journey. We're all set to go. Are you ready?"

"Of course. Let's go meet the people we'll travel with on this long journey."

Ellie and George found the group of wagons where the boy told them they would be. When they approached the camp, an older looking man with a long beard, dressed like a mountain man and sporting a mangled left hand, walked up to them, and said, "Howdy, I'm Tom Fitzpatrick, how can I help ya'll?"

"Hello, Mr. Fitzpatrick, we're here to go with your wagon train to California," George replied.

"It ain't really my wagon train, I'm only guiding three Catholic priests and a couple others to Montana. However, the party that is going further west has asked me to be their guide. You'll have to speak with John Bartleson, he's the one leading this venture,"

"Ah, all right. Can you lead me to Mr. Bartleson?"

"Sure. Follow me,"

"Sweetheart, do you mind staying with the wagon?" George asked Ellie.

"No, I don't mind, go on and do what you need to do."

Fitzpatrick led George through the assembled wagons and past the few dozen people who were engaged in various activities. Fitzpatrick asked, "You're Cherokee, ain't you? You sure look like one,"

George instantly became defensive. "Yeah. What of it?"

"No need to get riled up, boy. I know quite a few Injuns out west, like Flatheads or Cheyenne, and I ain't got a problem with nary a one. The few Cherokee I know are right fine people, so I wanted to let you know I don't have a problem with you being here. As for the others, who knows what they think. Probably think all Injuns are red-skinned savages and would scalp them if given the chance. Don't bring it up unless someone asks, because we don't need no trouble. All right?"

Sighing, George replied, "All right, Mr. Fitzpatrick."

"Good. Ah, look, there's Bartleson,"

Bartleson was writing something down, when Fitzpatrick said, "John, you've got another couple who wants to head to California,"

"Thank you." Turning to George, he asked, "Who are you?"

"I'm George Massey. My wife and I are looking to start our new lives together in California. I saw your advertisement about going west in my town's newspaper, so I thought joining your expedition would be the opportunity we're looking for,"

"I see. You're lucky to show up when you did. I don't have a problem with you joining us, but I do require a fee of one hundred dollars to join my group, which we call The Western Emigration Society. We plan on going first to John March's ranch in the San Joaquin Valley, then on to Sutter's Mill, where Sutter wants help from new settlers to build a community. Think you can pay the fee?"

George was surprised by the amount. *That's a lot of money. What's the saying? A fool and his money are soon parted. But am I really a fool for wanting to go west?*

Maybe, maybe not. Well, it's a good thing I have enough money. "Yes, sir, I believe I can." George took his billfold out of his jacket, opened it up, and handed the fee to Bartleson. "Here you go. Do we need to do anything else?"

"Thank you, good sir. No, I don't require anything else of you, however, make sure you're properly supplied for the trip as the places to supply on the trail are very limited. Please note that we're set to leave on May eighteenth. Understood?"

"I understand,"

"Good. Park your wagon next to the one over there," Bartleson pointed to a wagon to his left, "and then you can let your oxen or horses graze for the time being. Do you have any questions or concerns?"

"I don't think so, Mr. Bartleson."

"If you do later on, you know where to find me. Now, I'm busy, so if you don't mind, I need to continue with my work."

"Right. Thank you again, sir." George and Bartleson shook hands and George went back to Ellie.

On his way back to Ellie, George was joined by Fitzpatrick, who said, "I'm giving you a bit of a warning. That Bartleson fellow and most of those fools following him know very little about which direction they're supposed to go, but they're all convinced it'll be a grand adventure. He threw a fit two days ago about leading the train or else him and a couple of the men wouldn't go at all. As luck would have it, I showed up, and they asked me to guide ya'll for most of the way. If you want to back out now, I'm sure he'll understand,"

"Your warning is appreciated, Mr. Fitzpatrick, but my wife and I are determined to go west. Thank you for your concern. Now, if you'll excuse me, I have to move my wagon."

As George walked away, Fitzpatrick muttered to himself for what seemed like the umpteenth time, "Foolish people and their foolhardy ideas about the west. Someone's going to get killed one of these days."

When Ellie saw George, she asked, "How did it go?"

"The so-called captain of the wagon train agreed to let us go, but I had to pay a hundred dollars for the privilege. We're leaving on the eighteenth. He told me where to park the wagon, so we're going to do that right now,"

"All right. I think now would be a good time to get to know our fellow travelers before we venture off. I think it'll be exciting."

"I hope so too." George really did hope and pray the trip was exciting, but in a good way. He had a bad feeling that the trip could be worse than he could even imagine, so he tried to dismiss such melancholy thoughts. He knew in his heart that the Lord would protect him and Ellie from harm.

The wagon was parked in the spot where it was supposed to be. George unhitched the oxen and tied them to a picket line so they wouldn't wander off. Afterwards, the two young people prepared a campsite so they could sleep and eat before the wagon train departed. When they had some time, Ellie said, "I think I'll get to know the women that are on this journey. Are you going to meet the men?"

"I don't think so, at least, not right now,"

"Are you fine with me getting to know the people we're going to travel with?"

"Of course I'm fine with you doing that. Don't worry about me, all right?"

"All right. Love you." She kissed him and went looking for the women.

Ellie found six of them crocheting what looked like blankets. "Hi, I'm Ellie Massey. My husband and I are going west with your wagon train to California. Mind if I join you?"

"You're welcome to join us. I assume you know how to crochet?" asked one of the older ladies.

"Yes, ma'am."

"Good." The older woman handed Ellie crochet needles and showed the young lady where to start. The women got to know each other, but Ellie constantly worried about her husband being a loner, and wondered if he'd snap out of it as a business owner when they finally got California.

Chapter 15

Shortly before sunrise of the eighteenth of May, everyone in the wagon train woke up and went to work preparing their wagons for travel. Once the horses, oxen, and mules were hitched to their individual wagons or carts, Bartleson said, "All right, we'll be going northwesterly along the Missouri River, and then we'll follow the Platte for a while. Let's move 'em on out,"

"Excuse me, Mr. Bartleson, but shouldn't we pray first before we go anywhere?" asked one of the priests.

"Mr. DeSmet…."

"That's Father DeSmet to you," interrupted the priest.

Bartleson shrugged. "Sorry, I'm not Catholic. Does anyone object to him praying for the journey?"

Nobody said anything, although Ellie whispered to George, "What do you think? Should we object to him leading the prayer since we're not Catholic and we have issues with their doctrine?"

"Nobody really knows us, so I don't think we ought to rock the boat. When we're underway ourselves, I'll lead the two of us in prayer."

"Since no one objects, go ahead and pray, Father," stated Bartleson.

"O God, who did cause the children of Israel to traverse the Red Sea dry-shod. Thou who did point out by a star to the Magi the road that led them to thee. Grant us a prosperous journey and propitious weather, so that under the guidance of thy holy angels we may safely reach that journey's end, and later the haven of eternal salvation.

"Hear, O Lord, the prayers of thy servants. Bless their journeying's. Thou who art everywhere present, shower everywhere upon them the effects of thy mercy, so that, insured by thy protection against all dangers, they may return to offer thee their thanksgiving. Through Christ our Lord. Amen."

"Let's move on out, we're burning daylight."

"Boy, is that priest long-winded." Ellie whispered to George, who smiled at his wife's observation.

George made sure their wagon was the last in line and then he waited until the other wagons and the horse-drawn carts used by Fitzpatrick's party started moving before George led himself and Ellie in prayer. "Lord, we want to thank you for getting us this far. We pray that you continue to put a hedge of protection around us as we travel. I pray for our family back home that they continue to be safe, prosperous, and are able to live long lives. Thank you for our salvation and everything you do for us. In Jesus' name, amen."

The wagon train crossed the Missouri and followed it north until they reached the Platte. Days went by where nothing of significance happened. Occasionally, the men had to clear the land ahead of them of stones and rocks or fix the path they were on by filling in small gaps in the land so the wagon wheels wouldn't break or to prevent one of the animals from breaking a leg. Each time they stopped for the day, the wagons and the carts were circled together, the tongues of each wagon hitched to the back of the wagon in front, and then the animals were corralled inside. On a rotational basis at night, two men stood guard. Fitzpatrick warned, "Cook whatever ya'll's gonna eat before nightfall, then put out the fire. We don't want a fire blazing at night, that way we keep the danger from Injuns low."

Two weeks into the trip, the train reached the Platte. One of the men volunteered to go hunting. While everyone waited for him to return, Ellie said to George, "I can see why Stephen Long called this the 'Great American Desert.' It sure is flat, almost always dry and windy, even kind of brown and gray, with the occasional hill, and about the only trees are near the river. I can't imagine anyone wanting to live here or even being able to make a living here. It would be difficult to farm; the soil's too dry and doesn't look too fertile. At least they say California has tall mountains, rich soil, plenty of water, and lots of trees,"

"I don't know, the Indians who live in these parts seem like they have no problem living around here. Although, they follow the buffalo, so they probably don't worry about the soil,"

"I'm sure they're more suited to this environment than I am and they're welcome to it."

George wasn't sure he liked his wife's attitude about the land or the people who inhabited it, but before he could say anything, the hunter reappeared. He was on foot, without his horse, his pistol, and some of his clothes. Bartleson asked what happened, and the man shouted, "There's savage Indians out there! Thousands of 'em! They're coming this way. We need to get out of here!"

Hearing that there were thousands of Indians heading their way, a panic set in among the travelers and some whipped up their horses into a run, while those with oxen took a little longer to get their animals to start running. George wasn't sure what to do. Fitzpatrick knew he had to get the situation under control, so he chased after the lead wagon and managed to stop it, which had the effect of stopping the others. "No need to panic, just need to get this here wagon train in a square again, put the animals inside, and load your weapons. If'n those Injuns mean us harm, we'll soon find out, and if they do, we'll be prepared. Come on, hurry it up."

It wasn't very long before the Indians showed up, all mounted on horses, but significantly less than a thousand, because there were only forty of them. Fitzpatrick, Bartleson, and John Bidwell (the other half of the Bartleson-Bidwell Party) gathered together, and Fitzpatrick said, "Looks like they're a war party, but if they were hostile to us, they'd attack already,"

"But they stopped about a hundred yards from us and look like they're making camp. Maybe they're waiting us out and might attack us anyway. Mr. Gray did say they attacked him." replied Bidwell.

"We'll wait to see what they're up to. Since they're a war party, they can beat us and wipe us out in nothing flat. If nothing happens, I'll speak with them. All right?"

Bidwell and Bartleson nodded their agreement. Not too long after, the Indians set up their lodges for the night. Fitzpatrick went to Gray and said, "You and I are going to visit the Injun camp, we'll see what all this fuss is about,"

"Are you sure?" Gray was clearly nervous.

"If we don't, we sure ain't gonna be going anywhere. They might perceive the wagon train going on its merry way as a hostile act. Do you want us to be wiped out?"

"Of course not."

"Then let's go visit some Injuns."

Fitzpatrick walked the hundred yards to the Indian camp with Gray nervously following behind. One of the Indians, who looked like he was in charge, approached the two Americans with two of his own men. Fitzpatrick asked in sign language what tribe these Indians were from, why Gray ran, what happened to his horse and pistol, and why Gray returned with half of his clothes missing.

"We're Cheyenne. We were chasing down our enemy, the Pawnee, when our party came across this man out on the plains and it looked to us like he was doing a poor job of hunting, especially with such a tiny weapon. When we approached him, he became frightened and aimed his weapon at me. Because I meant no harm, I tried convincing him to lower his weapon. I don't know why, but he panicked and ran away. He left his horse and dropped his weapon, we don't know about his clothes. To show we mean no harm, we will return his animal and weapon to him." The leader indicated to one of his men to go retrieve the items.

When the man returned with the horse and gun, he handed the gun and the reins of the horse to Gray. Gray wasn't sure what to say, and having no knowledge of sign language, he nervously smiled. The Cheyenne warrior smiled back.

"Thank you for returning the horse and gun. We're in your debt." signed Fitzpatrick.

"You're welcome. However, remember this: we'll let your people go on their way, as long as you do not squat on our lands and kill most of our food. Agreed?"

"I agree. We're going west, beyond the mountains, and you'll have no trouble from us."

"Good. Starting tomorrow, for a short time, we will accompany you to make sure of this. For now, our business with you is complete." The Cheyenne leader and his men walked back to their camp.

"What did he say?" asked Gray when he and Fitzpatrick walked back to the circle of wagons.

"He said they weren't hostile and they thought you needed help. Next time, be more careful, because you have no idea which tribe of Injuns you'll come across. The Cheyenne are mostly peaceful to strangers, while there are other Injuns who will kill you for being a stranger on their lands and won't even bother to ask why you're there. Remember this and you'll do just fine."

"Them savages sure didn't look peaceable to me. Wouldn't it scare the tar out of you if they approached you with war paint on their faces and in that full battle get-up?"

"I suppose, but remember what I said about them not being hostile to you since they don't know you. You remember that and you'll keep your life."

Back in their own camp, Fitzpatrick told everyone what had actually happened and told them the Cheyenne wouldn't bother them as long as they kept going west, but would accompany the wagon train for a few days. Alarmed, Bartleson asked, "What about other Indians? Just because one group is peaceful with us, doesn't mean others are. How do we deal with them?"

"Don't get yourself all riled up over something that ain't happened yet. As long as we're not doing anything hostile, they'll leave us alone. I bet we'll be shadowed by many tribes along the way, but we'll never know they're there. Don't panic, that'll only lead to more trouble."

The next day, the wagon train moved on. The Cheyenne stayed with the train, but stayed ahead of them. Bidwell felt annoyed that they stayed with the wagon train and decided he would talk to George, since he knew George was an Indian. Bidwell dropped back to where the Massey's were, and said to George, "Hey, can't you talk to those Indians and find out what they're up to?"

"I don't speak the same language and I don't really know sign language,"

"Aw come on, aren't they your people too. I mean, ain't Indians all the same?"

"No, we're not. Are you the same as someone who's French or German?"

"Of course not,"

"The same is true of Cherokee and Cheyenne. Just because we live on the same continent doesn't mean we're related. Our people have two different cultures and languages, just like the French and Germans do. They're nomads, my people weren't. Now, do you still want me to speak to them?"

"Ugh, never mind." Irritated, Bidwell went back near the front of the wagon train.

George continued to walk beside his own wagon, satisfied that he had at least one person who might not still view all Indians as the same.

Another two days into the journey, the emigrants had to stop when a massive herd of buffalo going north to south prevented the wagon train from going any further. The sky was filled with dirt as the buffalo ran, the thousands of hoofs pounding the ground sounded like thunder to the Americans. The Cheyenne chased after the buffalo so they could feed themselves and their village. Some of the men on the wagon train took their single-shot flintlocks and began shooting at buffalo, taking down a couple. The Americans took some of the meat, along with the animals' fur, while the Cheyenne wasted nothing.

Seeing how wasteful the Americans were, the Cheyenne leader went to Fitzpatrick to complain, "Your friends are not taking everything from the animals. They kill too many and leave others to rot. My people take what we need and leave the rest of the buffalo alone. My people consider the buffalo a gift from the Great Spirit and we do not want to dishonor that gift."

Fitzpatrick said he understood and the Cheyenne leader left. The next morning, the

Americans discovered that the Cheyenne had disappeared.

The wagon train still had problems going any further. The buffalo herd continued to block their way. If it wasn't for Fitzpatrick and a dozen of the other men who had horses and shot their guns above the animals' heads to get the herd to move, some of the herd would've run over the assembled wagons and destroyed them. The herd also ruined the water in the Platte, because when they went through it, the water darkened, because of dirt, bugs, and whatever else had been sticking to the buffalo. Because of the water's condition, it became nearly impossible to drink.

George suggested to Ellie, "You could boil the water so we could drink it,"

"What good would that do?"

"Boiling it could make the water a bit easier to drink and you could also filter the bad stuff through some type of strainer, at least that's what my Ma used to do."

"All right, I'll try that."

Ellie first filtered the water through an improvised strainer, then boiled it, and waited for the water to cool off before she tried drinking it. She drank it and said, "It does taste better, not so gritty and smelling like every animal on Earth has swum through it. Thank you, Sweetheart."

Shortly before the wagon train left the High Plains, a thunderstorm formed above them. Heavy rain poured down on the travelers, the wind blew with gusto, and then hail the size of small stones began falling. The canvas tops on the wagons were torn to shreds by the hail and the emigrants had to hide under their wagons so they wouldn't get hailed on. Before too long, they saw a cyclone descend half a mile behind them out of the clouds. The funnel hit the Platte, causing the cyclone to turn into a water spout. Fortunately for the emigrants, the cyclone headed in the opposite direction. Unfortunately, they were stuck in mud until it dried enough to get the horses and oxen to pull the wagons out of it.

As they continued west, George complained, "I hope California's worth this trouble. Getting rain and hailed on, being stuck in the mud, being eaten up by bugs, drinking water unfit for even the animals, and putting up with this ridiculous weather that changes from hot-to-cold then back again is not what I had in mind. What was I thinking?"

"Dear, please don't be too hard on yourself, you wanted a new life for you and me. Sometimes, people have to go through hardship to get what they want. Although we're going through trials now and probably more until we get to California, we'll see our reward in the end and the Lord will provide."

"I pray that you're right."

Chapter 16

By mid-August, the wagon train finally came to Soda Springs, near Fort Hall, the location where Fitzpatrick's party would split with the main group, since his group were headed for Montana to meet up with the Flathead Indians. Along the way, they'd come across natural landmarks such as Court House Rocks and Chimney Rock, which to these easterners was a sight to see. John Birdwell took care to describe the details in the journal he'd been keeping since they left Missouri. Over the course of the three months, the wagon train had lost some horses to wandering young Indians, sometimes equipment ended up lost, one man accidently killed himself while cleaning his gun, and four others had either stayed at Fort Laramie or decided to go to Fort Bridger to wait for an opportunity to return east.

The travelers stopped at the springs to rest, which was along the Bear River. The day was almost perfect. Sun was shining, no clouds in the sky, and air temperature was in the upper seventies. As George helped Ellie get off their wagon, she said, "I've heard that the springs taste like soda water, because these springs are bubbly like soda water, which is why it's called Soda Springs. Let's go try it,"

Since George didn't object, Ellie grabbed his hand and they went down to Soda Springs. Kneeling down at the edge of the water, Ellie scooped up some water in her enclosed hands and drank it. "It does taste like soda. You have to try it, George,"

George kneeled down to try the water. His wife was enthusiastic when it came to trying new things, which made him happy that she was happy, but sometimes he regretted bringing them on this journey. Originally, he thought it would be a great adventure, they'd see new sites, experience new things, instead he felt like they experienced a lot of hardship. *Maybe Ellie's right, we have to go through this to get what we want. That's what I'm praying for anyway. I think all the Lord's doing is testing us to see if we really want to live on the other side of the continent from everything and everyone we know. We've made it this far, so it would be pointless if we didn't go any further.*

Sipping the water, George thought it tasted good and told Ellie so. She smiled, glad that her husband seemed to be enjoying something, then she thought, *He's been so lost in thought for so long and kind of melancholic. I know he thinks we made a mistake, but I can't help but see that this is what God wants for us. So what if we have problems along the way, stuff like that happens, we just have to work through the adversities of life, and I think we're doing that.* She prayed, *Thank you, Lord, for being there for us on this journey. Please continue to give us protection and we ask for traveling mercies. In your name, amen.*

When they walked back to their wagon, Ellie thought this was the perfect time to tell George some news she had. "I think you're going to be a father, my love,"

George stopped in his tracks, not sure he heard what he thought he heard. "What?"

Smiling, she replied, "I'm pregnant,"

"How? No, that's not it, I know how you got pregnant. Um, I mean when?"

"I haven't had my monthly for over a month and all the signs point to my being pregnant. We're going to be a Ma and Pa!"

Stunned, but happy by the news, George hugged Ellie and then kissed her. "When do you think he or she will arrive?"

"I'm not sure, probably around the beginning of next year,"

"Do I need to do anything for you that I'm not already?"

"No, Dear, you being here is more than enough. As long as I don't strain myself beyond my limitations, I shouldn't have a problem carrying our baby. Let's go tell the others."

The rest of the emigrants celebrated the announcement of the Massey's first child. The women gave all sorts of advice to Ellie and the men gave their advice to George. The young married couple felt overwhelmed by the advice.

After everyone rested for a few hours and explored the other springs in the area, Fitzpatrick gathered them together so he could speak to them. Once he was satisfied he had their attention, he began, "Now we come to the part of the journey where we split off. I know the way to Oregon Territory, so the trail is easy to follow. The path to California is relatively unknown and possibly difficult. With that in mind, I'd have no problem guiding all of you to Oregon, if you wish,"

A man named Amos Frye said, "I have no desire to wander about the countryside not knowing if I ever make it to California. If you guarantee getting me and mine to Oregon, I'll take you up on that offer."

From the shouts of agreement, it sounded like half of the emigrants wanted to go with Fitzpatrick. "I can guarantee I can get you there. And, from the sound of it, I think there's others who want to go with us.

All right, with a show of hands, who among you wants to go?"

Ellie turned to George and asked, "Are we going with the group to California or the ones who want to go to Oregon?"

"I think it would be best if we stick with our original plan,"

"All right, you're the head of our household, so I'll follow whatever you want us to do."

By the show of hands, Fitzpatrick's hunch was right – half of the people (thirty-two) in the wagon train wanted to go with him. He didn't have a problem with it, since he knew of trappers and other pioneers who got lost in the Rocky Mountains and were never seen or heard from again. Having gotten to know these people, he didn't want to hear about them dying from getting lost and dying of dehydration because they wandered into one of the deserts near the Great Salt Lake. But, if half of them were that stubborn, maybe they would get to California. "I see that just about some thirty odd people want to come with me. Good. We'll leave tomorrow."

"Fitzpatrick, I need to speak with you before you go," replied Bartleson.

"What can I do for you?"

"I'd appreciate it if you could give me as much detail about everything west of here that you know. Good spots for watering and spots to avoid, for example."

"Get me something to write on and I'll write down as much as I can remember. I'll even try to draw a map."

Fitzpatrick did his best to draw up a map and fill in the details from memory on the best way to get to California, but the map ended up being very vague. Since Bartleson had little idea on how to get there, Fitzpatrick hoped the other half of the wagon train made it safely. Once he finished the map, the mountain man said, "Here, I hope this does the trick. Best remember there's deserts and sandy spots out there where you can get lost and stuck. There's also Blackfeet out there who are hostile to strangers and wouldn't hesitate to kill ya'll if given the opportunity. If'n you follow this as best you can, ya'll should get to California before winter sets in. I also suggest sending a party to Fort Hall to get more information from the Army on what lays ahead, that information could be valuable. Got it?"

"I understand and I'll send a group. Should I wait here for them to return?"

"I think you ought to continue the journey. The men you send will be able to catch up to you later on. Do you got any other questions?"

"No, sir. Thank you for guiding us this far, Mr. Fitzpatrick. I hope God blesses you on your journey northward."

"I pray the same for you."

The next morning, seven wagons, plus the carts the priests traveled on, started north. Everyone said their goodbyes to each other, since the emigrants had gotten to know each other over the course of the last couple months. Some of the Oregon bound still tried to convince the California bound to go with them, but to no avail. The remaining nine wagons were pulled by a combined eighteen horses, oxen, and mules. The split party consisted of twenty-eight people, since Bidwell sent four men to Fort Hall because of Fitzpatrick's suggestion. The party continued on their journey. Before they started, Bartleson noticed Bidwell was gone, so he asked, "Does anyone know what happened to Bidwell?"

"While you were talking to Fitzpatrick, he and Mr. John said they were going hunting and fishing. They went west, towards those snow covered peaks. He said to continue without him and he'll catch up to us since he knows our route." replied Benjamin Kelsey. The Kelsey's were the only ones with a child that remained with the California group.

"All right, fine. We'll continue on. Let's get moving."

The wagon train continued on their journey. After about a day, they were beginning to wonder if the Blackfeet had killed Bidwell and John, until they saw the two emerge from the trees two days later in the middle of the afternoon. After nearly everyone in the wagon train greeted both men, Bartleson asked, "What took so long?"

"We nearly got lost. There were no trails where we went and wherever we walked was rough and rocky, which would've tore up our feet if we weren't more careful. We stumbled through thickets that were so dense we couldn't see the sun and we had to trudge through cold streams. We could tell bears and other wild animals were in the area, so we worried about being attacked. Last night, we even saw an Indian village in the distance and there must've been some of their scouts near where we were, because we found evidence of a campsite. We're both glad we're back."

The wagon train continued west and eight days later the men who went to Fort Hall caught up to them. They said the Army's advice was to continue going the basic direction they were going and they'd reach the Great Salt Lake, but were told to avoid going too far south, otherwise, they would reach country that had no water. The Army also said not to go too far north, they'd get lost in the mountains. They had to find a Mary's River that would lead them through the Sierra Mountains into California. No one in the party felt that the information was the least bit helpful, so they continued on their journey.

They finally reached the Great Salt Lake a few weeks later and found that most of the land surrounding them was a salt desert and the water in the lake was extremely salty. Because nearly everyone was exhausted from clearing rocks and other debris so the wagons could continue moving, and the animals were getting too tired to pull wagons because of their hunger and thirst for lack of their owners being fully prepared for the trip, Bartleson made a decision, "We're going to rest here for a few days and I'll send a couple of you to scout ahead. Everyone else needs to stay hydrated, even though the Great Salt Lake is salty. In order for you not to get sick, drink small amounts of it, like a handful every so often. If you try to drink it like regular fresh water, you will get very sick. All right, who'll volunteer to scout ahead?" Bartleson chose two men, the only two to volunteer, and both left immediately on foot.

While waiting for the two men to return, Ellie's positive attitude was nowhere to be seen when she said to George, "We're going to die, aren't we? Maybe we should've gone with the others to Oregon. We'll die out here, alone, and no one will know until they come across our bleached bones in this godforsaken desert,"

George hugged her. "I don't think we're going to die, I think God is still looking out for us. You said it yourself that you thought we'd have to go through some hardship before we found what we wanted. Looks like we're going through that now and probably won't be through it until we actually get to our destination. Please don't give up, I need you and I want us to have a family. Promise me you won't give up?"

"I won't give up, I'm just getting awfully tired of this journey. Maybe being pregnant alters my perception of things, but either way, next time we go on a long journey, let's go by ship."

"I think that's a good idea and we'll do that next time if we go anywhere. Now please rest while we're sitting here, all right?"

"All right. I love you."

"I love you too."

Five days later, the two men returned, and one of them said to Bartleson, "There's a little bit of grass for our animals to eat and passable drinking water a day's journey from here, otherwise, we're surrounded by desert. The mountains we're supposed to cross are far off in the distance,"

"All right, we'll head that direction. Let's go."

A day later….

"Is this all?"

"Yes, Mr. Bartleson," replied the man who told him a day earlier they found grass and water. He could tell Bartleson was disappointed.

What they found was what one would call an oasis, but it was a small one. There was barely enough grass to feed the horses, the mules, and the oxen, and barely enough water to let the animals drink and for the people fill up canteens. It didn't take long for the animals to eat up all the greenery and for the small pond of water to be used up.

"Now what?" asked Bidwell.

"I think we ought to abandon the wagons, pack what we can carry on the animals, and continue our journey on foot. I don't see any other way." Bartleson turned to the others and ordered, "All right, prepare your animals to be pack animals and pack only what's necessary. We're leaving our wagons here,"

Bartleson wasn't prepared for the anger directed at him, some of which had been boiling up since leaving Soda Springs. Some people had brought most of their possessions with them and were loath to give up nearly everything they brought with them. George was one of those unhappy with Bartleson's announcement. He went to Bartleson to complain, who was swamped with complaints from nearly everyone.

"I saved a lot of money to buy merchandise for a future store I want to open in California. I loaded my wagon with what I bought and if I abandon all of it, what am I and my wife supposed to do when we get to California?"

Bartleson heard the complaints, but refused to be moved from the order he gave. His response was, "I'm sorry, but no one told any of you to bring everything you owned on this trip. Once we get to California, you can rebuild your lives and buy new things. We need to get a move on, we can't stand here and argue all day, so get to work."

None of them, including George, had any experience with packing a load on horses, mules, or oxen. The animals were startled at first and a couple of the horses tried and succeeded in bucking off whatever was on their backs. Clothes were scattered across the ground as luggage crashed to the ground from the bucking horses, so attempts were made to make sure that it didn't happen again. After half a dozen attempts at trial and error, the animals were turned into pack animals. Now the emigrants all had to walk on foot, some of whom had shoes that weren't exactly made for walking long distances. The horses traveled faster than the oxen, so those with horses sometimes had to wait for the packed oxen to catch up. In spite of securing what they could on the animals, sometimes someone's things fell off and were strewn out behind them.

Weeks went by before the emigrants came across what eventually would be known as the Humboldt River, which was difficult to drink because the weather was turning from summer to fall and the river had become stagnant. Even though they now had barely drinkable water, they had run out of food days earlier. Antelope were hard to kill with limited range, smooth-bore, single-shot breech loading flintlocks and fish were sparse in the river, so the suggestion was made to kill an ox for food. They were down to eight animals now. All four horses, the four mules, and two of the eight oxen had wondered off or maybe were stolen during the multiple nights over the course of their walk across the future state of Nevada.

Attempts were made to find the animals, but eventually, it was determined no one should waste more energy trying to locate the missing livestock. The ox was killed for food, but only supplied the thirty-two travelers with food for three days.

It was late October before the emigrants finally came to the foot of the Sierra Nevada Mountains. For the majority of the time, they were lost. The last ox was killed for its meat and some of it dried so they could have a little bit to eat while trying to traverse the mountain range. After resting for two days, they began to make their way up and over the mountain range.

Chapter 17

The ragtag group of emigrants stumbled through the Sierras for two weeks before they found the Stanislaus River and then followed it to the San Joaquin Valley. They had great difficulty in finding enough food to eat and were almost on the verge of starvation when they finally found their way into the Valley. George, knowing more about hunting squirrels and other smaller game than the others, found enough to keep Ellie fed so she wouldn't lose the baby she carried and be malnourished. Sometimes he went without food, but made sure to eat enough to keep from starving to death. The Massey's didn't suffer nearly as much as the others because of George's ingenuity, but they were still hungry and tired. Luckily for all involved, it was in the fifties and sixties during the day and above freezing at night, so no one ended up with hypothermia. Finally, on November 4, 1841, nearly six months after the start of their journey to the west, they made it to John Marsh's cattle ranch.

Bartleson weakly knocked on Marsh's door. Marsh opened the door, was shocked when he saw the dirt covered, weak emigrants, and asked, "Are you John Bartleson and is this your Western Emigration Society wagon train?"

"Yes, sir. We finally made it here, but not without some considerable trouble,"

"I can see that. Before I ask you questions about why you're in such a state, I guess you and the others should come inside and we'll get you cleaned up and fed."

Marsh had enough room in his house for the thirty-two to get cleaned up. After everyone got cleaned up, his kitchen staff prepared a meal of deer, potatoes, and green beans. As they ate, Marsh began the conversation, "I was hoping to see healthy, prosperous settlers, not the bedraggled, poorly supplied settlers that arrived here. What happened?"

Bartleson explained everything that happened on the journey. Marsh listened to the tale, and said, "Since your group is one of the first that have traveled this far over land, instead of by sea, I can see being woefully underprepared. I'll let all of you stay here until you get healthy again, but you will have to go to the Mexican authorities in San Jose to get passports to be able to do anything here. Understood?"

"Yes, I understand. How far is San Jose?"

"It's a little over fifty miles south,"

"Oh." Bartleson wasn't thrilled they'd have to do more traveling, but they still had to go to Sutter's Fort, which was another week and a half worth of travel. "Thank you, Mr. Marsh for allowing us to rest here before we continue on."

"You're welcome."

When they were by themselves, George asked Ellie, "How do you feel?"

"I feel better now that I've eaten a full meal, not nearly as weak as I was starting to feel. I was afraid we might lose our baby if we stayed lost in the mountains too much longer and I thank God we found our way here when we did,"

"I'm glad we relied on God. If I had relied on Bartleson's word that we would eventually find our way, I would've feared daily for your and my lives. We should take a moment to thank God for getting us here,"

"Go ahead, Dear."

"Heavenly Father, we thank you for bringing us across this vast country safely. We thank you for our continued health and ask that we regain our strength to finally finish this journey once and for all. When the time comes, please give us a healthy baby. I also ask that you give me the wisdom to start a general store and please help me to be successful at the venture.

Thank you for everything you do for us. In your name, amen."

"By the way, when we're finally settled down, I need to write my parents and let them know we made it here safely."

By the beginning of December, the settlers were rested and now healthy enough to go to San Jose to speak to the Mexican authorities. Marsh let them borrow a couple wagons for them to travel in and they left at daybreak. They had to stop as night fell and were five miles from San Jose, so it wasn't much further.

Bartleson led the three wagons that Marsh loaned them into San Jose and headed for the local government building. The thirty-two headed into the building, but before they entered, Mexican troops surrounded them. A Mexican colonel came outside and said, "Search them for passports,"

"We don't have passports, that's what we were coming here for," responded Bidwell.

"No passports? All right, you're under arrest." In Spanish, he told the enlisted men, "Arrest them and put them in jail." Turning back to the Americans, he asked, "Who told you to come here seeking passports?"

"Why are we being arrested?" demanded Bartleson.

"You're here illegally. No passports, so you go to jail until someone can vouch for you. Do you have someone who can do so and did this person tell you to come here?"

"Yes we do. John Marsh, he's the one who told us to come here. He owns a cattle ranch just north of here,"

"Ah, we know of this Marsh. I'll order that he come here immediately. In the meantime, off to jail you go." The colonel ordered a rider to immediately ride to Marsh's ranch to retrieve the American land owner.

The settlers that signed up for the journey, long before Ellie and George joined up with them, griped at both Bartleson and Bidwell for leading them to yet another obstacle in their paths, complained that so far this was not turning out to be the paradise that both men described so many months ago, and were feeling cheated. The two didn't know what to say to refute their claims, but assured them that everything would work out when they least expected. Bartleson and Bidwell were upset with Marsh for allowing them to go to San Jose without him coming with them to vouch for them, otherwise, none of them would be in the situation they were in. Now, the only thing they could do was wait for Marsh to get them out of this predicament.

Marsh arrived the next day. When he stood in front of the Mexican colonel, he said, "Colonel Rodriguez, why do you have these people locked up? They came here to get passports, so that shouldn't have happened."

"They're locked up because they're here illegally. Can you vouch for these Americans before I give them passports? What kind of people are they? Are they hard-working people? Will they contribute to our society?"

"They are hard-working, family oriented, and faithfully follow Jesus Christ as their Lord and Savior. They come to California to seek a better life, will contribute to the success of California, and are law abiding citizens."

"There are no, how you say, agitators in this group who seek to overthrow Mexican authority like the Texians did?"

Marsh's answer was laden with sarcasm that the colonel missed, "No, of course not. They'll follow your laws." Thinking to himself, he thought, *If I have my way, we'll be out of Mexican authority soon and under American authority as soon as we can arrange it.*

"Very well, you've been a good citizen, so we'll grant these new settlers passports.

I'll go with you to order my men to release them."

Once they were released, Marsh said to them, "Now, for my trouble, I want five dollars from each of you,"

"What in Sam Hill for?" asked Bidwell.

"This business with you is taking me away from my business. My time is valuable and it's costing me money. I also expected healthy and well-fed settlers, instead I got you starving idiots which required me to spend more money to get all of you healthy again. If I don't get five dollars from each of you, I'll tell the colonel to keep all of you in jail. Do we have a deal?"

None of them were happy about his demand and were annoyed by his attitude towards them, but they agreed to give Marsh five dollars each. Except for George, who was prepared monetarily for the entire trip, the others were inching closer and closer to being broke.

"Now, are you staying in the area or are you going on to Sutter's?"

"We're definitely going to Sutter's. What would the best way to get there from here?" asked Bartleson.

"I suggest following the Sacramento River,"

"Where's that?"

"North of my ranch,"

"I see. How much would it be to buy outright the three wagons and the horses we used to get to San Jose?"

"Buying the horses and wagons are not necessary. I'll have my ranch hands retrieve them in January,"

"That's big of you," muttered Bidwell, but Marsh didn't hear him.

"Thank you, Mr. Marsh, because even though you didn't have to help us, you did. We'll be forever in your debt."

Yes, you will be and I'll come calling on that debt when the time comes. "You're welcome. Now, I have to return to my ranch. Good day and I pray God keeps you safe on your remaining journey." Marsh got onto his horse and rode away.

"Now what?" asked one of the settlers.

"We'll go to Sutter's. Since we're in town, does anyone have business to take care of, besides buying supplies?" asked Bartleson.

Ellie spoke up, "I'd like to send a letter to my family back in Kentucky to let them know we made it safely to California before we go anywhere else,"

"That's a good idea. If anyone else needs to take time to write letters, go ahead and do so while some of us buy supplies for the journey. We'll meet at the livery in two hours."

Those that were going to send letters all went to the general store to buy paper and one pencil for all of them to use. Ellie wasn't going to write a long letter until later, but did want her parents to know that she and George had made it to California. She wrote:

Dear Ma, Pa, and Jacob

George and I finally made it to California in November. The trip was long and perilous, as the man who said he knew the path here got us lost once we passed the Great Salt Lake. We had to abandon our wagon, along with the store goods that George wanted to use to open a store. However, it looks like there's a need for new settlers and George seems confident that he'll be able to do what he wants anyway. When we're finally settled in, I'll send you a longer, more detailed letter. We should be in Sutter's Fort whenever you write to us.

I also have some very good news – I'm pregnant. I believe I have two to three months before I give birth, so please pray that this child is safe and healthy and

that I'll have no ill effects from
the process.

We pray that this letter finds
you in good health and I miss all
of you terribly. May God grant
you everything you pray for and
I love all of you.

With love,
Ellie

The settlers gathered two hours later at
the livery. The wagons were filled, mostly
with food, the horses hitched to the three
wagons, and a prayer was said before they
began their travels. For what they hoped was
the last time, they began the one hundred
mile journey to Sutter's Fort.

A week later, they found Sutter's Fort.
The wagons stopped in front of the main
building, a two story adobe structure. Since
Marsh had been somewhat rude to them,
they half expected Sutter to be the same
way. Before going inside, Bidwell said to
the group, "All right, wait here, I'm going
inside to find out if Sutter's ready for us to
be here. It'll be a few minutes,"

Inside, Bidwell found a man working at
a desk, so Bidwell asked, "Excuse me, are
you Mr. John Sutter?"

"That's me. Who are you?"

"I'm John Bidwell, leader of The
Western Emigration Society. My group and

I have arrived here and we're looking to settle,"

"Welcome, welcome," Sutter shook Bidwell's hand with enthusiasm.

"You're glad to see us?"

"Of course. I was expecting you and your group. Let's go meet them, you can introduce me to them, and I'll show all of you around."

Sutter went outside, met with the group, and he was genuinely happy to see them. He gave them a tour of his fort, although it didn't take long. Sutter told them, "When I get enough settlers here, I want to call the settlement Neuva Helvetia, which means New Switzerland in English, since I'm originally from Switzerland. I want people to be farming, trading, and being involved in other forms of industry. I intend for my settlement to be the greatest city in all of Alta California. Now, all of you must be tired, so my people will help you find places to stay and will take care of your horses. I'm very glad to have you here."

A couple days later, George went to talk to Sutter about establishing a store in the area. "Mr. Sutter, I had intended to open a general store around here, so I started out with supplies to do so. Unfortunately, due to Bartleson's ineptness at leading the wagon train, we had to abandon our wagons and nearly everything on them. I was wondering if it would be possible to do what I originally intended?"

"I don't see why you can't. As you know, I plan on building a settlement, which I hope to turn into a city with considerable influence in California. I'll help you build this general store, just let me know when you want to start and I'll get my men to raise a building for you. I also have contacts with freight ships coming in from the Pacific, so when you need to buy anything, I'll give you those contacts. All right?"

"Thank you, Mr. Sutter." They shook hands.

"I have one other thing I need to ask about. My wife is at least five months pregnant, when her time comes to give birth, are there many midwives here who can help her?"

"There are. Many of them are either of Spanish ancestry or are Indians like yourself. The Indians are called the Maidus, some of which I have employed here. But, the two of you would probably prefer someone who speaks English, correct?"

"Yes, sir, an English speaking person would be more convenient, since neither of us knows Spanish or the local Indian languages."

"All right, I'll introduce you and your wife to a midwife before too long. Now, if you'll excuse me, I have other business to attend to."

Sutter did what he said he would do, and helped George build and supply his general store. George received the merchandise he needed to sell from freight ships coming from the ports of the United States that had to go around Cape Horn to get to California. His business grew as more and more settlers arrived in California, since Sutter's Fort was a waystation on the California Trail.

Four months later, April 1842, Ellie was ready to give birth. She found a midwife that was recommended and when Ellie went into labor, the midwife was called. The midwife was a Maidu and over sixty years old, but she had presided over many births in her adult years and knew English. A doctor was available in case anything happened that the midwife couldn't handle. George nervously waited for the birth of his first child as hours and hours went by, but no one told him anything, and he wasn't allowed to come into his house because the midwife had forbidden it.

Nearly a full day went by before the old Maidu woman gave permission for George to come into the house. George saw that his wife looked drained and was sleeping. His fear was that she would die in childbirth, but she didn't, so he silently thanked God. The old woman said, "She has twins,"

"What?"

"Your wife, she has two boys. She very lucky that she still lives and both are healthy. I go now, you visit with your wife."

George kneeled down next to the bed. Now he noticed that Ellie held two sleeping babies, while she looked peaceful in her slumber. George had lost track of the time when she finally woke, smiled at her husband, and said, "Congratulations, my love, you're a father,"

"And you're a mother, sweetheart. We have twins. Isn't that amazing?"

"Oh, yes, very much so. George, what do you want to name them?"

"Good question," George had no idea what to name the two boys, but two names popped into his head. "How about George Junior and Hopson?"

"Hopson was your father's name, wasn't it?"

"Yes. Do you mind?"

"Not at all. I'll love these two boys no matter what their names are. I love them and I love you."

"I love you and I love my two boys." George kissed Ellie and spent the next few

hours with his wife and new boys before he
had to go to work.

Chapter 18

American settlers in California began to overwhelm the mostly autonomous Mexican state's authority in almost a similar way to what happened in Texas ten years earlier. Now that James Polk was President of the United States, he wanted to acquire the Oregon, California, and New Mexico Territories. With his election, the United States Congress was urged to admit Texas to the Union, which it did, even though Mexico threatened war if that were to happen. In an attempt to prevent war, Polk sent a diplomat to negotiate and buy the California and New Mexico territories, while Oregon was British owned. In case Mexico refused, Polk sent troops under General Zachary Taylor to the disputed border region between Texas and Mexico. The war began May 11, 1846, after a reported skirmish between the Americans and Mexicans ended up with eleven American soldiers killed near the Rio Grande. Polk and Congress were also ready to go to war with England over Oregon, but both governments eventually worked out a solution since war between the two countries wouldn't be popular or economically feasible.

Before anyone in northern California knew about the tensions between Mexico and America, United States Army Captain John C. Fremont showed up at Sutter's Fort in December 1845, with sixty-two men. Captain Fremont's official reason to the local government for being in California was that he was on an expedition to map and explore the Oregon Territory. Unofficially, he was to get the American settlers to overthrow the Mexican authority, even though the United States agreed to a treaty in 1794 that said the United States couldn't wage war with another country they were at peace with. Fremont, if caught by the local authorities instigating an insurrection, could be court-martialed and accused of acting on his own without any authority from the American government. So he would try his best to make the local authority think it was the settlers' idea to revolt with no help from the United States. But before he could begin a revolt, Fremont planted the seeds of the idea in some settlers' heads. Unfortunately, he had to make sure he did what he was officially ordered to do, which was go on a mapping expedition so the local authority wouldn't be suspicious. He and his men supplied at Sutter's and made their way to Oregon for a short time. Fremont hoped that when he returned, the settlers were primed for what he wanted them to do.

When he returned to Sutter's Fort in late spring 1846, Fremont made it his headquarters. Once he established Sutter's Fort as an unofficial base of operations, Fremont reached out to the influential settlers in the area who were interested in California breaking away from Mexican control. Some of the settlers had already taken action, but in ways that had mostly annoyed the Mexican authorities. One of those influential people was John Marsh. He knew there were Americans who needed to hear what Fremont had to say. Specifically, it was a group of settlers that still owed him a favor and he decided now was a good time to cash in on it.

George was busy stocking his store the next morning when a customer came in. It had been four years since he'd seen the man, so George didn't recognize him at first. "Hello, Mr. Massey, remember me? It's nice to see you and good to see that you're doing well,"

"Sorry, sir, I don't recognize you. Who are you?"

"Don't tell me you forgot your old friend, John Marsh. You know, the one who fed and clothed all of you when you arrived in California and bailed you out of that jail in San Jose,"

"Oh, right. What can I do for you?"

"I'd like to invite you to go to a meeting that Captain Fremont is holding for us settlers. It probably won't take long, but you do owe me a favor and I'm cashing in. Other than Bidwell still living in this settlement, since he is the man who you order supplies from, do you know where everyone else is?"

"Sorry, we lost track of them two, maybe three years ago. As for going to this meeting with you, I'm busy,"

"You could get your wife to tend to the store or you could just close it for a while,"

"My wife is tending to two four year olds and a one year old, she can't help with the store at the moment. What's so urgent anyway that I have to attend your meeting?"

"I see. What's so urgent is that we're discussing who should be in control of California – Mexico or America. In my humble opinion we should be under American control and we plan on doing something about that in the coming days,"

"What makes you think I care? It doesn't matter to me at all,"

"You may not care, but you will if I tell Fremont that you're sympathetic to Mexico. He could toss you in jail and throw away the key once our little venture gets going. You wouldn't want your wife and children to be without you, would you?"

George frowned, he was in a no-win situation. "All right, fine, I'll go. Let me close the store first and I'll tell my wife I'll be out for a while."

"I'll be waiting."

George closed the store after Marsh stepped outside and then George went to his house behind the store. He found the two boys playing with their toys and the one year old daughter, Jenny, sleeping in the crib. Ellie sat next to the crib while reading *Oliver Twist*, which was a relatively new novel by Charles Dickens. She enjoyed Dickens, but his novels were too wordy for George, who wondered if Dickens got paid by the word. Ellie looked up, saw that her husband looked a bit worried, so she asked, "Is there something wrong?"

"I'm going to be stepping out of the store for a bit, so it'll be closed,"

"Why?"

"Do you remember John Marsh?"

"Yes, of course. He wasn't very pleasant when we last saw him,"

"Well, he thinks I owe him a favor since he bailed us out, so now I have to go to a meeting that Captain Fremont's holding,"

"Fremont's back? I've never met anyone so arrogant. I mean, just because he's done so much in our lifetimes and is related by marriage to an influential United States senator, doesn't mean he has to be that way. What makes him so special?"

"Yeah, he's back. I don't have the slightest idea why he thinks he's so special, probably because of those family connections back in Washington. I guess I'll go now, I'll be back later. Love you." They kissed and he left with Marsh to go to the meeting.

At the meeting, George saw a mix of regular settlers and men who were considered adventurers, somewhere over one hundred men in all. Some of the aspiring adventurers wanted to be like Kit Carson, who was also here as a scout and courier. George didn't see Bidwell or Sutter, since both men weren't too keen on overthrowing the local government, mostly because being aligned with the Mexicans had made them rich. Unfortunately, Sutter's influence with the other settlers was on the decline because of who everyone thought he aligned with, and no one thought he would change his allegiance unless it benefited him.

Once Fremont stood in front of them, the men settled down, and he began speaking, "Gentlemen, you know who I am. I'm here to encourage you to prepare for rebellion against the Mexicans. If you do so, my men and I will help you form militias so you can take on the local Mexicans, who don't look all that formidable and will probably fold easily. Any questions?"

"Yes, Captain. I'm William Ide. Do you have a strategy for us to battle the Mexicans?"

"That's entirely up to all of you. You know the lay of the land and what the Mexicans can field. I can loan you one of my men who can advise you, but he can do nothing else,"

"What about aid? Can you supply us with guns, cannons, and horses?"

"I'll do my best," was the weak response.

"What kind of answer is that?" asked Marsh before Ide could reply.

"That's the only answer I can give. This is supposed to be your idea. I can advise, but I cannot, according to my orders, engage the Mexicans. If I did help, I'd have to resign my commission so the United States government could disavow my actions. Now, will all of you help me to bring California into the United States?"

The room filled with chatter as the men discussed what to do. George listened, but didn't participate. After a few minutes of talk, Ide spoke up, "All right. We'll do it.

Some of us have been planning to capture a herd of one hundred and seventy Mexican owned horses. We heard reports that General Jose Castro was going to have the officer in charge of the herd have his soldiers use the horses try to drive us out of California. After that, we'll go to Sonoma, where arms and other materiel are stored. If we can deny them the horses and the materiel, maybe it'll go a long way towards our success."

"Good, sounds like a solid plan. Whenever you're ready to do what you need to do, I'll be here for whatever advice you need. Good luck."

Fremont left the group, while Ide and a few others began creating their militia. Marsh said to George, "What do you think? Do you want to join with us?"

Shrugging, George replied, "It really doesn't matter what I think, does it?"

"Not really,"

"As for joining, I have three children and a wife, I don't want to leave them without a husband and father if this whole venture goes south and Americans are kicked out of California because of the failure. After having nothing at one point in my life, I've worked too hard for everything to be taken away from me or my family. Not to mention the fact that I'm not allowed to be a citizen of either country. So, I will not join your campaign against the local Mexican authority,"

"I see you feel strongly about the matter,"

"I do. Have a problem with it?"

"Yes, but I understand your lack of enthusiasm, although I don't have to like it. However, if any of us find out that you decided to join with the Mexicans, there will be Hell to pay, not just for you, but your entire family. Understood?"

"I understand. Now, will you just leave me alone?"

"Very well. Goodbye, Mr. Massey, you'll not hear from me again."

George told Ellie what happened. She agreed with his decision not to join the rcbcls, although she did want California to be American territory and not Mexican.

The American rebels easily captured the horses owned by the Mexicans. A few days later, William Ide led thirty-three men to Sonoma, where they captured arms and materiel along with the retired Mexican general, Mariano Vallejo. Vallejo supported American annexation, but was arrested anyway. With this victory, they declared California an independent republic and proceeded to create a flag. Ide found a white sheet, had a grizzly bear drawn on it, with one red star next to it, and the words "California Republic" written underneath. With only a few minor skirmishes, the Bear Flag Revolt ended three weeks later when Fremont took over after supposedly resigning his commission and created the California Battalion out of the men who won the Revolt. The Republic of California ceased to exist a week later when they learned that Monterey had been taken without a fight and the United States flag was raised. The rest of the territory was also taken without much of a fight from the Mexicans. California was now a United States territory. The Treaty of Cahuenga officially ended the war in California.

Mexico surrendered a year later in the September 1847, after the United States occupied Mexico City with the defeat of the Mexican Army. With the Treaty of Guadalupe Hidalgo officially ending the war on February 2, 1848, the U.S. paid Mexico fifteen million dollars for all the territory it wanted, which amounted to five hundred and twenty-five thousand square miles.

Chapter 19

A week before the Treaty of Guadalupe Hidalgo was signed, a carpenter was working on a water-powered sawmill for Sutter on the American River near Coloma when he found flakes of what he thought might be gold in the river. Excited about his discovery, the carpenter told the others who worked with him what he thought he found, and then he raced to Sutter's Fort, even though it took him a day and a half on horseback to get to the Fort. Sutter was found at George Massey's store playing checkers with George. Sutter went out of his way to interact with all the business owners who lived in his settlement, so he could know who to trust. "Mr. Sutter, I found something you definitely need to see."

"What is it, Mr. Marshall?"

"Look," he showed Sutter the flakes of possible gold.

"Is that gold?" asked George.

"I sure hope so. I found it while I was building your mill, Mr. Sutter,"

"I'll have to test the flakes before we know for sure. If it is gold, and I really hope it's not, I don't want either of you telling anyone. Is that clear?" Both men said they wouldn't.

There were ways to test the gold flakes. First, Sutter found a ceramic plate and tried scratching the surface of the plate. The flake left behind a gold marking. Next, he retrieved a hammer so he could pound on the flakes. Since gold isn't brittle, but malleable, the flakes flattened and didn't break apart. The final test he conducted was using nitric acid, which cleaned the gold and got rid of all the imperfections that might've been in the flakes. It was definitely gold. Sutter wasn't happy with the results because he preferred his settlement stayed primarily agricultural.

Before he was able to do anything, Sutter was approached by Sam Brannan two days later. Brannan published the *California Star* newspaper, had his own store in San Francisco, and was a representative of the LDS Church in California. He was supposed to receive the tithes of the Mormon workers at Sutter's Mill and then send the tithes to Brigham Young in Utah. "Mr. Sutter, is it true?"

"What are you asking me?"

"Did your people find gold up at the mill?"

"Where'd you hear that? Did Marshall or Massey tell you that?"

"No, but one of your workers at the mill did tell me that Marshall discovered some flakes. So, is it true?"

Sighing, Sutter replied, "Yes, unfortunately. This discovery will ruin everything,"

"What do you mean? Discovery of gold will really put California on the map. We'll all be rich!"

"That may be true, but have you ever seen what happens to people when Gold Fever strikes them? All common sense goes out the window,"

"Who cares? This is the greatest news we've had in a while, I must report on it. I also think we're going to have need of picks, shovels and all sorts of other equipment to extract the gold, so I need to buy those too. We're going to be rich!"

The gleam in Brannan's eyes disturbed Sutter. It was the beginning of Gold Fever, which tended to make men greedy, suffer from an extreme lack of common sense, and even ignore their own health. Sutter didn't care about gold, but he knew others did and he knew that if word got out to the rest of the world, California would be forever changed. He wasn't looking forward to it. He also hoped that whoever did end up coming to California didn't end up like the Donner Party back in late 1846. Their stupidity had gotten them into major trouble, most of them died because of it, and he hoped gold seekers didn't end up like them. Sutter had personally seen what had happened to the Donner Party and wished that sort of misery on no one.

George decided to tell Ellie when they ate dinner, since he knew she wouldn't tell anyone else about the discovery and neither would their children. After praying over their meal, he said to her, "Looks like gold was discovered at Sutter's Mill,"

"Really? What does Mr. Sutter think?"

"He's not happy about it. He keeps saying he wants an agricultural paradise here, but he said that with gold being discovered, every Tom, Dick, and Harry will be all over the mountains and the rivers trying to search for riches. Maybe he's over-reacting?"

"I don't know, my father never went looking for gold, but sometimes he did wish he could find some. He said that if he did find gold, he'd probably succumb to something called Gold Fever, whatever that is,"

"Nobody in my tribe ever thought about mining for gold or even looking for it, but I heard my elders once talk about how white men found gold in the Carolinas about fifty years ago, and how crazy it made those men.

For some of my elders, it sealed their belief that white people were crazy. Maybe that's what Gold Fever is?"

"It might be. I know we're not poor, but we're not exactly rich either, so if you could, would you go looking for gold?"

"I don't know, maybe. If I do, I wonder if I need a shovel or something to find gold or randomly find it in a river like Marshall did? I guess I'll have to study on it while I'm working in the store. Besides, what's the worst that could happen with gold being discovered?" Neither could answer the questions, so they ate their dinner.

In San Francisco a few days later, Brannan began telling everyone he knew that gold had been discovered at Sutter's Mill on the American River. He was going to publish the news in his paper, but his staff left quickly for the Mill to find gold for their own. Brannan decided to buy up every pick, shovel, and pan to place them in his store so he could be the only one everyone had to go to. He bought the equipment for less than a dollar each, but charged fifteen dollars for each. Once he had everything ready, he went out onto the streets of San Francisco with a vial of gold in hand, shouting, "Gold! Gold on the American River!"

By the end of 1848 into 1849, news of the discovery of gold in California had spread across the world. Thousands of gold-seekers were running all over Sutter's land, destroying crops and ruining his dream. He discovered they weren't just Americans, but men from far-off places like Peru and China, that were mining for gold on his lands and in the rivers. To him, it seemed like some of the worst people in society had come to find gold, because even though there wasn't much crime at first, there was plenty of corruption and sin in and around the gold camps. Saloons and brothels always showed up wherever fortunes were being made. There was also plenty of diseases because of lack of proper sanitation and diet. The whole business disgusted Sutter.

Sutter's oldest son, John Junior, came from Switzerland the same year to help his father manage New Helvetia, but instead saw the possibilities for the commercial use of the land. The younger Sutter decided to build a new town called Sacramento because of the Sacramento River. His father wanted the town to be called Sutterville, but the son wouldn't listen. Because his dreams were being ruined and it was making him go into debt, the older Sutter decided the time was right to sell New Helvetia.

"Mr. Brannan, I can no longer keep New Helvetia going from all the money I owe, because none of my workers want to do anything but look for gold, so I'm selling off my land and other assets. Would you be interested?"

Brannan had become richer than he'd ever imagined from selling supplies to the gold miners, plus reportedly being accused by his own church of using church funds for himself, so he was thrilled when Sutter asked, "Of course I'm interested. Does your other assets include the fort, plus all the buildings on the property?"

"Yes,"

"Excellent. We'll go to my lawyer and draw up a contract. You've made the right choice, Mr. Sutter."

"I pray to God that it is."

Meanwhile, George had yet to take the time to search for gold, mostly because he wasn't very interested and the way people acted because of it disturbed him. About the only thing a lot of the customers in his store could talk about was gold and what they would do if they found some. George developed the ability to tune it all out because the sheer greed bothered him.

In the early months of the Gold Rush, some of the men were ill-mannered toward his wife whenever she was out by herself, mostly because she was attractive and they seemed to lack the social graces most people usually learned as children. George was angered by this, but Ellie downplayed the various incidents because she didn't want trouble from the men or for George to get into trouble with the law.

One morning, George saw Ellie come out of the Post Office only to start being harassed by two men, dressed like miners, and it enraged him. So to protect his wife's honor, George went over to two, and ordered, "Leave her be!"

"Who are you?" one of them asked as he spit tobacco on the ground.

"He's a savage Injun, that's what he is." replied the other one.

"I'm her husband, that's who I am. Now, are you going to leave her alone or do I have to make you do it?"

"There's two of us and one of you. Go ahead and try to make us."

George answered by wailing into the two men and taking them on all by himself. Ellie watched her husband with tears in her eyes, worried about him getting hurt, but proud that he was willing to protect her even when the odds weren't in his favor. George got his share of punches, but held his own, and looked like he was winning the battle. The town's sheriff came to see what was going on, watched George take on the two men, so he asked Ellie, "What happened?"

"Those two men were harassing me, so my husband decided to do something about it,"

"I see. So, it's a matter of self-defense. Would you like to press charges against them?"

"I don't think so. Maybe they'll learn not to harass women from now on because one never knows when a husband will come out of nowhere to protect her. But you ought to do what you need to do, Sheriff,"

"I will. They could probably use a night or two cooling down in a cell. Looks like your husband has won the fight. I'll collect the two and haul them off."

After only ten minutes of fighting, George was bloodied and bruised, but he managed to beat the two men. Ellie took him back to the store so she could fix him up. He wasn't too injured, so he continued operating the store. The sheriff arrested both men and took them to the jail. The tale of what George did spread and the other miners left Ellie and other women alone.

The reason for Ellie being in the Post Office was because she had received a letter from her parents. It was also the same day Sutter had decided to sell to Brannan. Communications were becoming faster and she hoped that one day the telegraph would reach all the way to California so she could send letters faster, or maybe the Post Office would invent a way for mail to transverse the country even faster. In the letter, which had been sent only two weeks ago, her Ma wrote:

Dear Ellie, George, and my grandchildren,

I pray that this letter finds you well and happy. Tell the children their grandma and grandpa say hello. I saw in the paper that California is having an economic boom because of the Gold Rush. I pray that God blesses you from the fortunes being made and you don't have to live your life worrying about money.

I have some good news. Jacob, as you know, ran off to join the war with Mexico, even though he was only sixteen at the time. He finally returned to us back in June. He had some stories to tell about his adventures, and luckily, he suffered no injuries or even contracted a disease. I thank God every day that Jacob's returned.

Although, he has gotten it into his head to join the regular Army since he still thinks of it as a grand adventure. Please pray that he changes his mind.

Now I have grave news. Your father suffered a heart attack a week prior to this letter. He was working in the fields like he always does, even though Doctor McReynolds told him last year that his heart was no longer up to the task, but you know your father, thinking he knows more than the doctor. Doctor McReynolds thinks he'll die soon and that I need to think about giving up the farm. Thomas and Jacob are helping the best they can, but they can only do so much. Please pray for your father and me while we go through this because I don't want to lose him. If you're able, I pray that you can see your father before he goes.

I love you,
Ma

The news that her father was dying caused Ellie to cry. The children tried comforting her, but it made them upset to see their mother crying, so before too long, the three were crying too. George found them crying when he closed the store for the day. Concerned, he asked, "What's happened?"

Ellie handed him the letter. He read it and felt grief for his in-laws. They'd taken him in when they didn't have to and he was forever grateful to them for doing so. He wasn't sure what to do now, because they didn't have enough money to travel cross country again and there was no one to take care of the store while they were away.

Hugging Ellie, he said, "We ought to pray that God provides us a way to return east, because we don't have the means to do so at the moment,"

"All right. Children, let's join hands as your Pa prays."

The five joined hands while George prayed, "Lord in Heaven, we come to you today to ask for help. Duncan, Ellie's father, is dying and we'd like to visit with him one last time before he dies. We have no way to return to Kentucky, so we're asking that you provide a way. Thank you for everything you do for us. In your name, amen."

The next day, George had a visit from Brannan. Brannan came into the store and asked, "Are you George Massey?"

"I am. Who are you?"

"I'm Sam Brannan, owner of the *California Star* newspaper, the Brannan hardware stores, and other properties. I am also the new owner of the land and assets previously owned by Sutter, including the land beneath your store. I'm here today to talk to the owners of all the businesses here at Sutter's Fort,"

George wasn't sure he liked the direction the conversation was headed. "How can I help you, Mr. Brannan?"

"I want to discuss a buyout with you. How much would you like for your store? I want to expand into general merchandise, but I don't want to compete with you,"

"Are you serious?"

"Very. How much would it take to buy your store? Would three thousand do it?"

"Three thousand dollars?" George was astonished, he never had that much money at once.

"That's what I said. That offer is on the table for three days. After three days, my offer will continue to go down and I would have no problem crushing you as competition. However, I would prefer buying you out instead of ruining you. Once you decide, we go to my lawyer so we can make this legal. What's your answer?"

"Would you mind if I talk to my wife first? I'd like her opinion before I answer,"

"All right, but you have still have three days,"

"I don't think it'll take that long. Can you wait while I go get her?"

"Fine, but making me wait costs me money. Hurry it up." Brannan made a show of looking at his pocket watch.

At the house, George found Ellie, and said, "I think our prayers are answered,"

"What do you mean?"

"You know the newspaper man, Sam Brannan? He bought up Sutter's assets, so now he owns everything here. He offered to buy the store for three thousand dollars. We can go back to Kentucky without worrying about how to get there or how to pay for it. I think I know you answer, but I'll ask anyway. Do you think I ought to sell?"

"Oh, praise the Lord for answering our prayer! Of course I think you ought to sell. Is Mr. Brannan still here?"

"Yes."

"Let's go talk to him,"

George and Ellie went back to the store hand-in-hand. Brannan was impatiently looking at his pocket watch when the couple came back. "So, what's the answer?"

Smiling, Ellie replied, "We accept the offer."

Chapter 20

After signing the contracts that Brannan's lawyer had them sign, Ellie and George wondered what to do next. So they discussed how they would go east. The children were at home, being watched by the woman who was the midwife at their births.

"I remember you saying that if we ever went back east, you'd want to go by ship. Do you still want to do that?" asked George.

"I don't know. Have you seen or talked to the people who have come off those ships?"

"No. What's wrong with them?"

"All of them end up very sick. One woman, who was one of the few who came with her husband by way of ship from New York instead of by land to look for gold, said that it was easy to get sick and stay sick on the journey. They ended up with scurvy because of the lack of vegetables, the food was moldy and filled with bugs, they lacked fresh water, and they had seasickness from the rough, stormy seas. I even heard that the trip could be anywhere from six to eight months, depending completely on the sea conditions. I still dread going overland though, especially with a desert east of the

Sierras, and our options are limited with three children,"

"No matter what we do, I don't think we'll get to Kentucky in time if your father dies before we get there,"

Tears streamed down Ellie's cheeks, and she replied, "I know and it hurts to think about that. I can send a letter telling them we're on our way and it'll get there ahead of us. I wish there was a faster mode of transportation, but there isn't, so we're stuck,"

"I've seen the pamphlets that were based on the memories of the men who have returned east from California or Oregon that people used as maps to travel on the trails. Unfortunately, one of those was by Lansford Hastings. His map was what caused the Donner Party to have their problems, so we won't use it. Maybe we can hire someone to guide us back to the more heavily traveled Oregon Trail,"

"I think that's a brilliant idea, George, and we won't get lost that way. Do you think we ought to take furniture with us or leave it with the house?"

"Leave it. Brannan has the house too, so let him deal with it, we can always buy more furniture later on. You know, maybe we should talk to the Army about guides that will get us as far as Fort Hall. If we can get an arrangement, we'll go buy the wagon and supplies, all right?"

"All right, let's go."

George and Ellie went to the Presidio in San Francisco, which was the United States Army Headquarters in California. In the administration building, George and Ellie were directed to a lieutenant who would know such things. "I'm Lieutenant Conroe, how can I help you?"

"Hello, Lieutenant. Um, we're planning on returning east and would like to know if there's some way we can hire a guide that will take us as far as Fort Hall?" asked George.

"Normally, I'd say we could do that, but that's not possible right now. You see, we're having problems with the Mormons. They've claimed the territory the United States bought from Mexico for their own and have said that it's their land of Deseret. They've put tolls on the roads and trails that people have been using to go to either California or Oregon. They've also burned down Fort Bridger, so the Army's been tasked with putting down this insurrection. I'd say it's currently not safe for travelers to be going through that area,"

"We discussed going by ship, but that's just as perilous, since it takes more than six months and goes around Cape Horn,"

"You know, it's not necessary to go all the way to Cape Horn now. You see, in Panama, they've built a railroad that goes across the land, so if one were to use that shortcut, they no longer have to trudge through rivers and the jungle to get to the Gulf of Mexico. There's also less risk of developing yellow fever, malaria, or cholera, plus getting bitten by bugs, snakes, or any number of nasty creatures if one traveled on foot through Panama. From San Francisco to Panama is two weeks, and the shortcut should take about two or three days,"

"That's good news. Do you know if we can go directly to New Orleans to catch a steamboat instead of having to go all the way to New York?"

"I'm sure that can be arranged,"

"Who do we need to speak to for travel arrangements? We have children, so we need to find a ship that'll accommodate them too," asked Ellie.

"I can direct you to the right ship captain, just give me a second and I'll write down the name of the man you need to see. He and his ship should still be at port here in San Francisco for a few more days. Tell him I sent you and he should be willing to help," he handed George the name of the captain and the ship he commanded.

"Thank you, Lieutenant, you've been a help." replied George.

"You're welcome. If you need anything else, don't hesitate to ask."

At the port, George and Ellie asked about where to find this captain and the ship. They finally found someone who knew where the captain and his ship was, so they went to the pier where the ship was moored. They found the large, three-mast ship and a few men from it working on or near the ship, so George asked if he could speak with the captain. One of the men said he would go get the captain. A few minutes later, an older man approached George, and asked, "I'm Captain Fredrickson, how can I help you?"

"Captain, I'm George Massey and this is my wife, Ellie. Lieutenant Conroe at the Presidio sent us. We're seeking passage on your ship. We want to go to Panama, where we'll board the train that'll take us to the Caribbean. Can we arrange a trip on your ship?"

"Yes, I can take you there, for the price of three hundred dollars,"

George looked at Ellie with a questioning look on his face. Ellie shrugged, and said, "We have the money, George,"

"I know, but three hundred seems like an awful lot,"

"Mr. Massey, I charge three hundred because my ship is a merchant ship, and every passenger I carry is less cargo I can carry, so the price is how I make up for it. Since the Gold Rush began, I've had to alter how I conduct my business. Do we have a deal or what?"

"I have a couple questions first before my husband agrees to this. First, we have three children. Would they be a problem for you and your crew?"

"No, ma'am, as long as you keep them out of our way,"

"Good and we'll make sure they'll stay out of your way. Secondly, we've heard of people having health problems on board. So, will being on the ship for two weeks affect us in any way?"

"Seeing as you're our only passengers, you won't have a problem, since the ship won't be crowded like it was on the trip here. Since it'll only take two weeks to travel to Panama, the food or water won't be a problem. You may have problems with seasickness though, so be aware of that. Do we still have a deal?"

"Yes, I suppose we do," George shook Johnson's hand and handed him three hundred dollars.

"All right, good. We have a tight schedule, so we leave in three days at sunrise. Will you be ready by then?"

"Yes, we only have to pack our clothes, get our children used to the idea, and we'll be ready to leave by then. Thank you, Captain."

"You're welcome."

George and Ellie returned home. Their children were happy to see them. George Junior had been reading *Frankenstein*, even though he and Hopson were only eight years old, but he was a very serious and studious boy who enjoyed reading. Hopson was playing outside. Hopson was usually a stubborn, rebellious child, so he got spanked a lot, but he was also a boy who liked exploring the world around him, which caused him to have all sorts of scrapes, bruises, and broken bones. Both boys definitely looked like their father, but weren't identical twins. Jenny, who was only five, looked a lot like her mother, and was a very friendly, talkative child, although she had to warm up to people first before she talked people's ears off. She was playing with her dolls when her parents came home. Once the sitter was dismissed, George and Ellie had the three sit down at the kitchen table so they could tell them the plan.

"Children, we're going to go to move to Kentucky, where your grandparents live," George said.

"How come?" asked Junior.

"Well, Ma and I sold our store and the house because your grandpa, your Ma's Pa, had a heart attack, and he's not doing well. I think you'll be interested to know that we're going by ship,"

"I'm sorry grandpa isn't feeling good, and I think going by ship would be interesting, Pa,"

"How big is the ship? Will we get to see whales and sea monsters? I think it would be neat if we did," asked Hopson.

"I guess it's pretty big, it has three masts. We probably won't see sea monsters or anything,"

"Oh."

"What do you think, Jenny?"

The little girl shrugged her shoulders, kept combing the hair on her dolls' head, and said, "I'll go any place you and Mommy go."

"I'm glad you three don't have a problem with the idea. Now, we need you to pack your clothes and one or two toys since we can't take too much on the journey, all right?"

The children understood and excitedly went to their rooms to begin packing. Ellie helped Jenny, who was unsure of which doll to take, and was upset she couldn't take everything. George packed three books with his clothes, while Hopson packed only his clothes, figuring he would have fun on the ship and would have no need for toys. Ellie wrote a letter to her family and sent it before leaving for the ship.

Before getting on the ship, George had the family clasp hands, and he prayed, "Dear Heavenly Father, we ask today that our journey is a safe one and ask for traveling mercies. Please guide Captain Frederickson and his crew and give them the wisdom they need to traverse the ocean. Please help us as we travel across Panama and then back to the United States. Thank you for everything you do for us. In Jesus' name, I pray, amen."

The journey on the boat was relatively quiet. No storms tossed the ship about, the food was up to par, and the water stayed fresh. Over the two weeks, Hopson got into trouble for pestering the ship's crew with questions about the ship itself, like how the sails worked when it was a steamship, and just generally being in the way because he looked for whales and wanted to know if there were any sea monsters. He was disappointed when he saw no whales and was told sea monsters were myths. Junior and Jenny kept to themselves and obeyed their parents, while Hopson had to be disciplined a couple of times for disobeying. The only time anyone got sick was the first few days when George suffered from seasickness, but he eventually got over it.

Two weeks later, the ship docked at the port in Panama City. The Massey family left the boat and headed for the railroad depot to buy tickets for the trip from Panama City to Aspinwall (Colón to the natives), the port city on the Caribbean. Aspinwall was the last name of the man who owned and operated the Panama Railroad Company. At the ticket office, they were told, "The railroad is still being worked on, so you'll probably end up traveling on the Chagres River until you get to Aspinwall. From there, a steamship should be able to take you to New Orleans. Tickets to travel on the railroad are twenty five dollars."

"This will be the first time any of us have seen a train or been on one and I'm looking forward to it," said George.

"I think we're all excited, Sweetheart. Aren't we, children?" Ellie asked the three. The three were practically bouncing off the walls with excitement.

The train consisted of the engine, followed by a coal car, two cargo cars, and then two passenger cars. As the train made its way across Panama, the family could see that huge swaths of jungle had been cleared and the railroad workers were still working on the tracks and the land near the tracks. The land the tracks sat on had to be constantly maintained because of the huge amounts of rain Panama received each year and some of the land used to be mostly swamp, so the tracks occasionally began sinking when there was too much rain. Bridges were under construction to counter the problems. However, the engineering required to build these bridges for the tracks to eventually go on made the work slow, and even slower with constant rain. An hour into the trip, the train had to stop because work was still being done ahead. The train company loaded everyone onto a steamboat on the Chagres River and sent them on their way to Aspinwall. Because they stayed inside the boat, the Massey's avoided being eaten up by bugs, but were occasionally bitten by mosquitoes, fortunately, none of them ended up sick as a result. They also had never seen so much rain in their lives, as rain fell at least every half hour. A few hours later, the steamboat arrived in Aspinwall. George got the family tickets on a steamship that would stop off at New Orleans before continuing on its way to New York. Another week and a half and they'd finally be in Kentucky.

Chapter 21

A month earlier….

Out in his field, Duncan and his horse were plowing up one of the fields for planting. It was a hot, humid, cloudless day, and Duncan was feeling his age. Doctor McReynolds had been telling him to start taking it easy, but Duncan was being his usual stubborn self and was not listening to the doctor. Moira tried to get her husband to listen, but he thought he knew best. Two hours into plowing, he felt a sudden pain in his chest, one so bad that it caused Duncan to pass out, and collapse to the ground. Luckily, the horse stopped and waited for his master, not knowing that the human wouldn't be getting up for a while.

Jacob was doing his own chores, helping his parents catch up with everything after he had run away to join the Army when the United States went to war with Mexico. For him, it had been a wondrous adventure, albeit fraught with danger as most soldiers got sick from various diseases instead of dying from wounds in battles. He had met up-and-coming officers, like Ulysses S. Grant and Robert E. Lee, and was very impressed by them. The Mexicans weren't up to the fight and the Americans had taken the capital city of Mexico with not too much trouble. Jacob thought it a shame that Mexico wasn't part of the United States now, but he understood, but didn't care about, the political ramifications of why the government hadn't done so. It was because of the balance of power between the industrial north and the slave-owning agrarian southern states, at least that's what the newspapers and abolitionists claimed. Jacob figured he'd let the powers-that-be worry about such matters.

He was tending to his own matters when Moira came to him, and said, "Lunch is almost ready, go tell your Pa to stop and come to the house to eat. Okay?"

Wiping the sweat off his brow, he replied, "All right, Ma."

Jacob walked out to the field where Duncan was, which took ten minutes. When he got to the edge of the plowed up portion, he saw only the horse at first, he felt troubled by the fact that his father didn't seem to be anywhere in sight, so he went to investigate. Jacob found his father lying on the ground and apparently unconscious. I pray to God he's not dead, thought Jacob as he reached down to check his father's pulse on his neck. While the heartbeat was erratic, Jacob could feel it beating through the vein on Duncan's neck. Thank you, Lord! Now I just need to get him back to the house. So how do I do that? Jacob decided to unhitch the horse from the plow, picked up Duncan, laid the older man across the back of the horse, and then started for the house.

Nearing the house, Jacob called for Moira, "Ma, come out here, quickly!"

Moira rushed out of the house, saw her husband on the back of the horse, and the thought ran across her mind that he was dead. She began crying, "Is he dead? Please Lord, no!"

"No, Ma, he ain't dead, but he is unconscious. We need to get him inside and I'll go fetch the doctor. Okay?"

Rattled by seeing her husband in such a state, she replied, "Yeah, all right, um, go get Doc McReynolds. Please hurry!"

After setting Duncan on his bed, Jacob went to the barn for the other horse, didn't bother saddling him, but did put the reins and bit on so he could control the horse, and hurried for the doctor's office. A few minutes later, hoping Doctor McReynolds was his office, instead of out on his rounds, Jacob jumped off the horse and went into the office. He found the doctor in the office.

"Doc, you need to come with me, I found my Pa out in the field unconscious,"

"All right, let me get my medical bag, then we'll go to the stable where my horse and buggy are, and we'll head on out to your place. I told your Pa to take it easy, but would he listen? No, he's too stubborn to listen." McReynolds grabbed his bag. "Okay, let's go."

Back at the McGregor farm, McReynolds examined Duncan the best he could with the current medical equipment he had. Duncan woke up shortly before McReynolds' arrival, but was in a weakened state. After the examination, McReynolds took Moira and Jacob aside, and said, "I believe he had a heart attack, a massive one at that. I'd give him a few weeks or less to live,"

"So he is dying?" asked Moira, who had exhausted her tears and looked like a woman who'd been crying for a while.

"I'm afraid so,"

"Is there anything we can do for him?" asked Jacob.

"You can keep him comfortable, but don't let him exert himself, it'll only make things worse. I'm sorry, I wish there was more that I could do,"

"You did what you could, Doctor, thank you. Would you like to pray with us that God will prevent Duncan from suffering while he lays dying?" asked Moira.

"All right."

"Jacob, would you lead us in prayer?"

"Okay, Ma. God in Heaven, we come to you this day with heavy hearts. My Pa, Duncan McGregor, is dying from a heart attack. We ask that in his last days he doesn't suffer any pain, but is comfortable. Please guide my Ma and me through this difficult time and give us the wisdom to do what's right. Thank you for Doctor McReynolds and please bless him as he continues to minister to the sick. Thy will be done. In your name, amen."

After the doctor left, Moira said to Jacob, "I'm going to write a letter to your sister telling her about what happened. I need you to tell Thomas and Laura what happened and then send a telegram to Caleb about your father. Can you do that for me?"

"I'll do that for you, Ma, and I'll go to town as soon as you write the letter."

Jacob sent the letter and telegraphed Caleb the sad news about their father. Thomas and Laura closed their store for the rest of the day and Laura would stay with Moira for the time being. A few hours later, Caleb replied in a telegram that he and his family would head for Kentucky as soon as they could.

Three weeks later, Moira received Ellie's letter, and she was happy with the news that Ellie, George, and the children would be returning to Kentucky. Moira decided to read the letter to Duncan, even though he spent most of the time asleep as he got weaker and weaker, losing lots of weight in the process. "My dear husband, we received a letter from Ellie. She says they're returning to see you and hopes and prays that you get better. Isn't that great news?"

Moira saw Duncan faintly smile as he took his last breath and died. She burst into tears, while Laura sat by her, crying too. The two were still crying nearly half an hour later when Jacob heard the crying when he came into the house and he saw his father had died. He cried with them for a short time, before he said, "I'll go to Mr. Brown, the undertaker. He has some coffins already made, so I'll go get the coffin, and we'll bury Pa under the Oak tree next to the house. Okay, Ma?"

"All right." she replied through the tears.

Jacob took the wagon to town and went to Brown's business. Brown had already prepared a coffin for Duncan, so Jacob paid for it, and loaded it on the wagon. Before returning home, Jacob went to the church to ask the new pastor, Micah Grant, to officiate over his father's funeral. Pastor Bowen had retired a year earlier.

Jacob found the preacher at his desk, studying the Bible, and writing some notes, so he asked, "Pastor, are you busy?"

"I'm preparing for Sunday's sermon. How can I help you?"

"Well, my Pa just died and I wanted to know if you would officiate over his funeral?"

"I'm so sorry to hear about Duncan. You have my condolences. Yes, of course, I'll do that. When will the funeral be?"

"I suppose we should do it day after tomorrow. Can you do that, Pastor?"

"I can. Will it be at the cemetery?"

"No, sir, we're going to bury him on our land, under an Oak tree,"

"All right, I'll be there. Tell your Ma I'm praying for you and your family and let her know that Duncan is now safe at our Lord's side in Heaven. Please also tell her that I'll come by the house later and discuss with her the funeral service and whatever else she needs to discuss with me concerning Duncan. Okay?"

"I will and thank you."

Two days later, the funeral was held on a sunny, cool day. The friends of Duncan and Moira who were still living in and around Paducah were there, but Ellie and Caleb's families were not able to attend. Pastor Grant began, "We have gathered here this afternoon in God's presence as family and friends to remember the life of Duncan McGregor and to commend his soul into the gracious care of our Lord and Savior, Jesus Christ. We come together in grief, acknowledging our human loss. May God grant us grace, that in pain we may find comfort, in sorrow we find hope, in death we find resurrection.

"The Apostle Paul writes in the Holy Scriptures that the joy of the Lord is our strength. Proverbs reminds us that a merry heart is as good as any medicine. We remember Duncan as a strong man of faith, a man who adored his family, and would do whatever he could to protect his family. He was a loving husband, having been married to Moira for forty years. When he was ten years old, Duncan accepted Christ into his heart and did his best to live as a Christian for the rest of his life. Duncan and his family attended church every time the door was open and gave of his tithes faithfully. His children saw how he lived his faith, so all four accepted Christ as their Savior when they were young and are still faithful in their worship.

"Duncan was a friend to those who wanted one and would help out a neighbor when asked with no reservations. He was active in the community and was known for saying what he thought, even though it sometimes got him into trouble. Although he was born in Scotland, and only arrived in these United States at a young age, he was a very patriotic American, more than many who were born here, and loved his adopted country. Duncan had a sense of humor that would cause many to laugh alongside him and the stories he told about the Old World made many eager to listen.

"Now we come to Duncan's committal to the earth for his burial. For as much as it has pleased Almighty God to take out of this world the soul of Duncan McGregor, we therefore commit his body to the ground, earth to earth, ashes to ashes, dust to dust, looking for that blessed hope when the Lord Himself shall descend from heaven with a shout, with the voice of the archangel, and with the trump of God, and the dead in Christ shall rise first. Then we which are alive and remain shall be caught up together with them in the clouds to meet the Lord in the air, and so shall we ever be with the Lord, wherefore comfort ye one another with these words.

"After saying our finals fare-wells, let us go forth in the certain hope of being reunited with Duncan at the end of time. Go forth with God's peace and may the Almighty bless you now and forevermore. Amen."

The coffin was lowered into the ground. When the coffin was firmly in place, Moira, Jacob, and Thomas each poured dirt over the coffin. Later on, when the other mourners went home after the post-funeral reception, Jacob and Thomas finished burying the coffin under the dirt and then placed the gravestone at the head of the grave.

Chapter 22

Before they left New Orleans, George found out they could send a telegram to Paducah so Ellie's family would know they were on their way. He said in the telegram that they arrived in New Orleans, would be on a steamboat, and would arrive in Paducah in about three days, depending on the speed of the boat and weather conditions surrounding the Mississippi River. The telegram was sent off and the family made their way onto the boat. The children were fascinated by the steamboat, along with all the other boat traffic on the Mississippi. They even got to see how the ship's crew found out how deep the water was and kept the ship from running aground or into sandbars.

Three days later, on a warm, sunny day, the steamboat arrived in Paducah and docked. As they left the boat, Ellie saw her three brothers waiting for them. She felt dread for the news that she felt was sure to come from her brothers, so she took George's hand, and both led the children to see their uncles.

"Welcome home, we're happy ya'll made it," said Thomas in an almost sad tone.

He hugged his sister, shook hands with George, and mussed up the hair of the three children.

"I'm glad to be back. I hate to ask this, but is Pa dead?"

"Yes, he died last week, right after receiving your letter. I'm sorry,"

Ellie had been preparing herself for the bad news ever since receiving her mother's letter, but it still hit her harder than she expected. She embraced her brother's one by one while crying and cried for five minutes before stopping. They talked while they walked to Thomas' wagon, which they would use to take to the farm.

"How's Ma?" she asked while wiping away her tears.

"She's mourning, but Pa had been growing weaker every day since his heart attack before he passed peacefully in his sleep. Ma said she felt at peace with his eventual passing two weeks before he died since she would see him in Heaven when she died. Laura, Sarah, and our children are with her right now,"

"I wish we could've gotten here sooner,"

"I know, but Pa understood why it would take you so long to get here. Please don't beat yourself up over it,"

"All right,"

"So, these are your young-in's?" asked Caleb.

"Oh, yes. Children, meet your uncles: Thomas, Caleb, and Jacob. Brothers, this is George Junior, Hopson, and Jenny,"

The children were shy around their uncles, while the three uncles were happy to meet their nephews and niece. The eight got onto the wagon and made their way to the farm. On the way there, George asked, "How's your parents' finances?"

"They're not in debt, but we're going to have to discuss what to do with the farm, since Ma can't take care of it all by herself. Unless, of course, you and Ellie decide to take it over," replied Thomas.

"Ellie and I haven't really discussed what we're going to do. We've been worried about your parents the whole trip here, so where we're going to live or if we take the farm is something that we'll discuss later,"

"Jacob, do you still have plans to join the Army full time?" asked Ellie.

"I can't say for sure, Ellie, my plans are still up in the air. I don't want to take over the farm, that's too much work for so little return on the investment. Maybe if we sold all but two acres of it, Ma could still live there, grow a garden for herself so she could have vegetables, and also grow some fruit trees too,"

"You know that's Ma's decision, not ours. We shouldn't pressure her into doing something that she'll regret later," said Caleb.

"Caleb's right. For now, we support and comfort her the best we can. No more talk of this subject unless Ma brings it up, all right?" Thomas, being the oldest, told his siblings. They agreed.

When the wagon stopped in front of the house, Moira had been waiting for them on the porch in her black mourning dress, as was Laura and Sarah, and their children were off playing somewhere. As soon as George and Ellie's children got off the wagon, Moira introduced herself, hugged the three, and they hugged her back, happy to see their grandma. George and Ellie approached her, hand in hand, and after hugging both, she said with tears in her eyes, "I missed both of you so much. I'm glad you came, and I'm sorry you weren't able to see your Pa before he died,"

"We missed you too and I'm sorry we didn't make it in time, but we tried. How are you doing, Ma?" asked Ellie.

"I'm sad, but I'm also happy to know that I'll see Duncan in Heaven when I die. I want you to know that he was proud of both of you for not giving up when you went cross country into the unknown and he thought that it was very brave. You'll have to tell us about your adventures and your trip back as soon as we all get settled. Now, before we do anything else, I think we should pray and thank God for bringing George, Ellie, and the children back to us, safe and sound. Thomas, would you do the honor?"

"Lord, we thank you this day for bringing George, Ellie, and their children safely back to Kentucky. Please give them the wisdom to do what they're supposed to do next as they travel through life. Please help our entire family as we go through this difficult time. Thank you for everything you do for us. In Jesus' name, amen."

After everyone settled down and the children were put to bed, George and Ellie regaled the family with stories about their long journey on the Oregon/California Trail, what California was like, what the war with Mexico was like in California, and the Gold Rush. Next, they told what it was like on their trip from California to Panama back to the United States. George said, "I don't want to ever go to Panama again. It was hot and humid, more than anything I ever experienced in Georgia. It rained a lot too, maybe every half hour or so, even though we were only there for a day. And then there were the bugs after the rains. In some places, the bugs were so thick, you couldn't see the sky. Occasionally, it seemed like night because there were so many,"

"You must be joking about the bugs," replied Thomas, trying to suppress a shiver. He hated bugs.

"Maybe, maybe not. Do you want to go there and find out?"

"No thank you!" The adults laughed at Thomas' response. After talking for another few hours, the adults all went to bed.

A few days later, after Caleb and his family went home to Texas, and Thomas re-opened his store, Moira asked Ellie, "So, daughter, what do you and my son-in-law plan on doing when it comes to where you live and where he works?"

"I really don't know, Ma. Money currently isn't an issue for us since Mr. Brannan gave us three thousand dollars for the store. George was thinking about investing some money in the stock market, on something like the telegraph or a railroad company, or maybe buying bonds. He says he'll have to eventually speak to a banker about what to do. George really doesn't want to be poor ever again and have people push him around. He still wants to own a general store, but where at, he doesn't know right now. As to where we live, we haven't discussed it yet. We were going to ask you what you plan on doing with the farm, but didn't know when and if we should ask,"

"I've been thinking a great deal on the subject since none of my children are farmers, nor do any of you want to be. I could sell off all but one acre, keep the garden I currently grow anyway, and buy the meat and other foodstuffs from stores or others who raise and sell beef. What do you think?"

"I think you need to do what's best for you, Ma. Have you told the others what you want to do?"

"Yes, your brothers don't have a problem with the idea, especially since Jacob had been hinting at it for a while. Your father and I built this place from the ground up and it really hurts that I'll have to give a lot of it up, but it's more than I can handle by myself. I'm sure there's people out there looking for land to buy, so I don't think the land will be up for sale long. Now we just have to figure out how much to sell it for."

It didn't take long for the land to sell. A young family from New York bought the land for five thousand dollars and Moira had to get used to living on one acre. She was happy that she wouldn't have to rely on her children for money, since five thousand dollars could go very far in the 1850's.

Meanwhile, the children of George and Ellie were experiencing what their parents experienced shortly before they went west and were still experiencing as they discovered, prejudice towards them. This time, it was from the children they went to school with, along with some prejudice from their teacher. Hopson, being the one who always seemed to find trouble, found himself in more trouble one day when he had more than enough of being picked on. George Junior and Jenny endured the bullying, saying almost nothing to their parents about it, but Hopson tired of always turning the other cheek.

"Hey, savage Injun, you gonna scalp me today?" asked another ten year old boy, Hiram Darby, while the kids were on recess.

"Leave me alone, Hiram,"

"What's the half-breed gonna do? Huh?"

"I'm warning you, Hiram, you better knock it off,"

"Oh, I'm so scared," Hiram stuck his tongue out at Hopson.

That was exactly the wrong thing for Hiram to do. Hopson lost his temper and threw a right hook at the other boy. Hiram was hit in the eye, he stumbled, but stayed on his feet, and retaliated with a punch to Hopson's stomach. Hopson doubled over for a second or two, then jumped on Hiram, sending both to the ground, where they rolled around, punching each other. As they fought, the other kids gathered around the boys to watch them tear each other apart, and encouraging the boys to keep fighting. Junior and Jenny stayed near the schoolhouse. Jenny was scared for Hopson and cried, so Junior held his sister's hand to try to comfort her as they watched the fight.

"Ma and Pa are going to be really mad at Hopson. Ain't they, George?" asked Jenny.

"I guess, but I can't say for sure. I hope Hopson beats the tar out of Hiram."

"Me too."

Their teacher heard the commotion. So he went outside, saw the fight, and waded through the children to see who was fighting. With no effort at all, he picked up both boys, and demanded, "All right, who started the fight?"

"He did!" The boys exclaimed at the same time. The two were bloody and bruised, while their clothes were dirty and tore up.

"Hopson, did you start the fight?"

"No, Mr. Stewart, Hiram started it. He was calling me a savage Injun,"

"Hiram, did you call Hopson a savage Indian?"

"Well, ain't he?"

Sighing, Mr. Stewart knew he had to punish both boys, but one more than the other. He didn't want to take Hopson's side, since some of the children would tell their parent's about what happened if he did, and then the parents would demand the town council find another teacher. He couldn't stomach losing his job over some half-breed. "Boys, both of you will stand in a corner until the end of the school day. Afterwards, I'll send for your parents, but both of you will stay in the corner you're in until I speak to them. Now go."

George and Ellie were told what happened when Junior and Jenny came home from school, how it really wasn't Hopson's fault, because the other kid started it with the name calling, so they went directly to the schoolhouse. Hiram's parents had already come and gone, so the Massey's wouldn't have to deal with snarky remarks from Hiram's father. They saw their son still in the corner, while Stewart was at his desk, grading papers.

"Mr. Stewart, we're here. What would you like to talk to us about?"

Stewart didn't bother to get up from his desk to properly greet George and Ellie. "Mr. Massey, Hopson is a troublemaker and we need to do something about it,"

"Like what?"

"I'm going to suspend him from school,"

"Why? What about the other boy? Did you suspend him too?" Ellie asked.

"Hiram's been taken care of. Hopson causes too much of a distraction, since he likes to cause trouble, so that's why I'm suspending him,"

"Is it because he's of mixed heritage? Junior and Jenny told us what Hiram said to provoke my son, so I really don't think Hopson's the one you should worry about," replied George.

"It doesn't matter who was wrong. Most of the townsfolk with children aren't too happy I let your children come to this school and I'm getting threats about it. So, suspending Hopson is the best option,"

"I see. I suppose protesting to the school board will be pointless?"

"More than likely."

"Fine. We're done here, Mr. Stewart. Hopson, come on, let's go." Hopson left the corner, stuck his tongue out at his teacher, and the three went home.

On the way home, Ellie asked, "What are we going to do?"

"I have an idea, but I want to get home so we can discuss it with Junior and Jenny too."

At home, which was Moira's house, George had his wife and children sit down at the table to discuss possible plans. When they were ready, he began, "I think it's time we move on,"

"Why? Where would we go?" asked Ellie.

"The people who were here when we got married are still hostile towards us and aren't exactly secretive about it. Now our children are being bullied by the children of some of those same people. As for where we should go, I think we ought to go to Indian Territory, where the Cherokee are, to be exact,"

"Why there? Wouldn't they be hostile towards us too?"

"No, because they have no problem with mixed marriages. Chief Ross, for example, is a product of a mixed marriage. His father was a Scot and his mother was Cherokee. The Cherokee Council even passed a law in 1825 that treated children like ours as Cherokee. Although, we don't belong to one of the seven official clans, so I really don't know how that would work. What do you think?"

"I suppose we could try. I'm tired of the hateful looks we get when we're in Paducah and the occasional hateful remark thrown our way. Children, what do you think? You might find friends in Indian Territory that you don't seem to have here,"

The only response the three gave were shoulder shrugs and "I don't knows."

"All right, I think we should go as soon as possible, since we're not tied to a house or a job at the moment. I'll find out when the next steamboat is supposed to make a stop at Fort Smith and then I'll get us tickets." replied George.

A week later, the Massey's headed for Indian Territory to begin another adventure.

To be continued in *A House Divided*, a novel that will start off shortly before the Civil War and will follow what happens to the Massey's during the Civil War. One of the sons will join the Confederates, while the other will join the Union.

Other Works (go to cliffball.net for more info)
The End Times Saga Series (Christian fiction)
Times of Turmoil
Times of Trouble
Times of Trial
Times of Rebellion
Times of Destruction
Times of Judgment
Times of Tribulation
Jon Ryan (short story)
Xavier Doolittle (short story)
Standalone Novels/Short Stories
Beyond the New Frontier
Out of Time
Shattered Earth
Voyager and the Aliens
Dust Storm (Christian fiction)
Future works (as of mid-2015)
A House Divided – book 2
The Falling Away (first novel in new series)

About the Author

Cliff Ball is a Christian, lives in Texas, has two BA's, and a Technical Writing Certificate. He won third in a youth magazine for a short story he wrote through Creative Writing class in high school back in 1992, called "Role Reversal." You can visit his website at cliffball.net for more information about Cliff's novels, check out the blog, chapter excerpts, reviews of his books, and where you can find him on social networks.

47736217R00155

Made in the USA
Charleston, SC
16 October 2015